NORTH OF
BIG SPRING

NORTH OF
BIG SPRING

JOE WAYNE BRUMETT

TATE PUBLISHING & *Enterprises*

Published by Tate Publishing & Enterprises, LLC
127 E. Trade Center Terrace | Mustang, Oklahoma 73064 USA
1.888.361.9473 | www.tatepublishing.com

Tate Publishing is committed to excellence in the publishing industry. The company reflects the philosophy established by the founders, based on Psalm 68:11,
"The Lord gave the word and great was the company of those who published it."

Book design copyright © 2009 by Tate Publishing, LLC. All rights reserved.
Cover design by Kandi Evans
Interior design by Joey Garrett

Published in the United States of America

ISBN: 978-1-60696-493-4
1. Fiction / Christian / Historical
2. Fiction / Romance / Western
09.02.23

DISCLAIMER

All the characters in this book, with the exception of a few historical and military civil war characters, are fictitious. Any resemblance to actual persons, living or dead, is purely coincidental. Big Spring was a big spring, and the author used some of the history of the spring. The town of Big Spring used in the book is a town of the author's imagination, and should not be construed to be the modern city found at that location today. This is a work of fiction. The events described here are imaginary.

DEDICATION

To my wife, Martha Ann, for her loving, caring, and sincere ways; she is a genuine Christian, mother, and wife, who has the spirit of God in her life, and spreads that spirit to all about her in song and by example. I dedicate this book to her.–JWB

ACKNOWLEDGMENTS

To Dan Brumett and Tom Brumett for their help in marketing my book. Tom Brumett, my nephew, worked several long hours changing my manuscript from Microsoft Works to Microsoft Word. Tom got my manuscript to Tate Publishing Company.

I thank my granddaughter Marti Henry for her assistance with my computer. If I needed advice, Marti was available and saw that the problem was solved.

My thanks to Tate Publishing Company, and to their excellent personnel; I highly recommend them to all authors. They were patient with me, as this was my first book.

IN THE CIVIL WAR

The night was extremely dark with the moon hidden by an over-cast sky; the hour was late. I rode up the lane past the row of slave dwellings that bordered the north side of our dirt lane. A few coon dogs tied out back let their masters know that an intruder was riding up the lane. Shep, ever the guard dog, joined in with his angry remarks, which changed to yelps of pleasure and greetings as I called his name.

The main house of the plantation was a three-story frame dwelling with large clapboard siding and double-hung windows adorned with large, green shutters. The roof was tin and painted dark green. Five large columns supported a front porch across the front of the dwelling, and English boxwoods and a stone walk off-set the mansion from the lane. The lane turned toward the east side of the dwelling and led to the main barn approximately a hundred yards to the north.

I was weary; it was several hours past my bedtime, and my horse seemed eager to get to the barn. I patted her and spoke words of love and affection. My horse, Jane, was a grulla (blue horse) and had been named by me when she was a new colt and I was only fifteen. Though the night was hot, I hadn't ridden her hard enough that she should be rubbed down. I simply took off the saddle, saddle blanket, and bridle, and turned her into her stall. I climbed the ladder and, in the darkness, found the hayfork and threw her some hay from the hayloft. I went through the back door into the kitchen area of the main house.

"That you, Tom? What time is it?" my dad called from the top of the stairs.

"Where've you been, Son? I was worried about you!"

"I was at Wilson's Tavern with Bill Deane, Bill Runyon, and Ralph Smith. They drank a little, but I didn't. They're all heated up about the news and are considering joining the Confederate army. I heard that Colonel James Lawson Kemper of Madison is forming a brigade and that several have already enlisted. Boy, am I tired. Can we talk of this in the morning?" I pleaded.

"Here's the Richmond paper; there's an article there on the front page that'll interest you," said Dad.

He stood in his nightshirt in his bedroom doorway and held a kerosene lamp. He looked tired and a bit wobbly; I could hear him wheezing, and the sound was dry and harsh. He had been under a doctor's care and had consumption.

The paper fluttered as he coughed with a deep rasping sound. His left hand went to his chest, and then he reached for his handkerchief. Still, he clutched the paper and extended it to me.

"Dad, are you all right?" I asked. "You want me to mix some of that brandy and honey as a cough syrup for you?"

"No, Son. I'm just hot, as there is very little breeze, and I've an extra touch of hay fever. Let's both get to bed, and we'll talk in the morning."

•

It was a beautiful April morning as I crossed the random-width heart-of-pine floors of the hallway and passed into the dining room, where Goldie Williams was serving Dad and setting a place for me. "Thomas, you wash yo' hands while I fry yo' eggs. Do you want three or fo'?" she inquired.

I held up four fingers as I passed her. I went into the kitchen, where I pumped cold water into a pan and added some hot water from the tea kettle. Goldie brought the eggs, grits, biscuits, and bacon, and watched me as I bowed my head to thank the Lord for my food. Buck Williams stood smiling and filled my cup with coffee.

Dad sat at the table stirring a cup of coffee with a newspaper in front of him, obviously waiting to finish the conversation we'd started the night before.

"Tom, look as this paper and especially this article," he said, pointing to the article he placed before me. "Lincoln Issues a Call for 75,000 Men." The article was dated the fifteenth day of April 1861. I stirred my coffee and read to myself. *President Abraham Lincoln issued a call for seventy-five thousand men to form a militia. The troops will come from each of the Northern states remaining in the Union. Those called will serve for a period of three months. Should people question the reason for the gathering of these troops?* President Lincoln then made the following proclamation: *I deem it proper to say that the first service assigned to the forces hereby called forth will probably be to repossess the forts, places, and property which has been seized from the Union.*

"He is kinda sure of himself, is he not, calling for only seventy-five thousand troops and for only three months?" I said, smiling. My eyes crossed the page of the newspaper as I spoke. "Dad, did you see this? Twiggs Surrenders." I pointed to another front-page article and continued to read about how Brigadier General Twiggs, who commanded the Department of Texas, had surrendered all the troops under his command to the state of Texas. Various forts in the seceding states had also capitulated, and over three thousand big guns had fallen into Confederate hands.

There was an article describing Fort Sumter. It had been built on an island composed of rocks and stone. The fort lay on the south side of the channel to Charleston Harbor. The shape of the fort was pentagonal and constructed of solid concrete in three stories. The building was under construction, and only seventy-eight of the total one hundred thirty-five guns were in place at the time of the fall of the fort. I folded the paper, took a drink of my coffee, and sought the attention of my dad.

"Dad, when I was so late last night, Ralph Smith, Bill Deane, Bill Runyon, and I'd been meeting with Second Lieutenant Warren G. Jenkins of Company A of the Seventh Infantry under the command of Colonel Kemper. Warren had just joined the brigade and been commissioned. Several from this area are enlisting, and the four of us plan to go to Madison tomorrow to join."

I lowered my eyes as I spoke, not wishing to see the disappointment on my dad's face. After a full minute, my dad spoke.

"Son, I know Colonel James Kemper well, and he can get you a commission."

I had finished primary school in Lexington, Virginia, and had completed some military schooling at Virginia Military Institute as a preliminary for entry at West Point. Dad was especially interested in West Point and had approached our senator for my possible enrollment. I'd completed three years at Virginia Military Institute and knew that Colonel Kemper was a graduate of that institute.

"Dad, I don't think I'm ready for a commission; I would like to soldier together with my friends. The lieutenant stated that I'd make a good drill sergeant, and he said he would talk with Colonel Kemper about that possibility. With all of that marching at the institute, I think I can handle being a sergeant. I think that this uprising will be over before the snow flies."

"Maybe by the end of this we can all get back to normal, and you can finish your schooling at West Point," Dad spoke softly. "Son, spend the day getting ready. I won't stand in your way."

•

Our volunteer group was formed with several recruits from Orange and Madison counties; all together we became a part of Company A of the 7th Infantry, Kemper's brigade, later Pickett's Division, First Army Corps. Because of my military schooling, I was appointed a first sergeant. I began drilling and working my squad from morning till night. I taught various formations and commands that troops would need on the battlefield. We drilled and worked with calisthenics to toughen and harden the squad. It was hard at first, as we had a very warm April, but we all wanted to be good soldiers, and soldiering was new to most of us.

The firing line was much different, as the Orange boys, as well as our neighbors from Madison, could tear the center out of the target at one hundred yards. Some could do well at two hundred yards, and their shooting improved. My squad was given special attention, as we became quite deft in our drilling, and our officers looked on us with pride. I must admit, it was the training I received at Virginia Military Institute that should have the credit, but the officers were looking at me as officer material.

We marched to Culpeper. It was there that we learned that the Yankee Congress had passed a bill calling up five hundred thousand recruits. This was about July 1861, and right then we knew that this war would last longer than first thought, and that we would not be home, as I told Dad, "before the snow falls."

Many of our troops were dressed in gray uniforms, and many wore homespun uniforms stained with butternut. This butternut stain gave us the name "butternuts" later in the war. At Culpeper, we watched General Jeb Stuart direct his cavalry through their drills. Colonel James Lawson Kemper saluted our company as we marched in review, and my squad brought smiles to our colonel as we marched in special formations. He had invested deeply in his brigade and paid for much of our supplies and guns.

We camped on the edge of the town of Culpeper and were near a stream in the northern part of the town. A lot of attention was being paid to our cavalry. General Stewart had a young officer by the name of Pelham, who was raised in Culpeper. He would later command Stewart's artillery. General Longstreet brought up the rest of our division from Gordonsville, and it appeared that we were ready to show the Yanks what we Southern boys could do.

Several of our volunteers were a little concerned about a bayonet charge. We had never been shot at, nor seen an enemy squad with "fixed bayonets" advancing toward us across a field.

"I don't like that cold steel. You can't see a bullet, but that bayonet being thrust at your stomach isn't a delightful thought. Fellows, stand close to me and don't let me run!" said Bill Deane from Orange, a good friend that I had known all my life.

"You'll do all right. Just defend yourself as you've been taught, and save your load in your gun to fall back on. If you stick your enemy and you can't retrieve your bayonet, just pull the trigger and the bayonet will be blown out," I instructed.

Bill Deane got a little green and turned away from me.

The Yankee army was coming out from Washington to meet us.

They came with cannons and wagon trains as well as some cavalry. Both armies were in poor physical condition, and the weather was extremely hot. The Northern army had left Washington at two o'clock in the morning, and coordination between their advance troops and wagon train caused a bit of delay. They weren't prepared for attack as their general wanted, and the delay angered him. A large crowd of senators and members from the House of Representatives, along with their ladies and friends, had been given special permits to watch the coming battle. They sat in their carriages with umbrellas to ward off the July sun and awaited the thrashing of the Southern farm boys. This "picnic affair" was an aggravation to the advancing military generals from Washington.

The Union troops had marched twelve and a half miles that morning and were not hardened physically for such a march. They went right into battle. There were thirty-four thousand men in the Union army, but a portion, Runyon's division, was left to guard the lines of communication back to Washington. The Confederate army consisted of twenty-eight thousand men and forty-nine pieces of artillery and a battalion of cavalry. Both armies met on the banks of Bull Run, a stream near the town of Manassas.

General Longstreet's troops awaited the advancing Union ranks and met Tyler's division at Blackburn Ford. This was on the eighteenth, I believe, and we were there at Blackburn Ford under Colonel Kemper. We were fighting on a plateau with the Yanks, trying to find a ford to cross Bull Run. The Yanks appeared to be getting the best of the battle, and we were retreating. There in the midst of our retreating Southerners stood my professor from the Virginia Military Institute. "Look!" cried one. "There stands General Thomas Jackson just like a stonewall." The terminology held, and General Thomas Jackson became "Stonewall" Jackson.

We faltered until reinforcements poured onto the field from the South and saved the day when the balance of General Johnson's troops, that had arrived by train, were immediately rushed into battle. We fired volley after volley of musket rounds into the advancing Northern army, who broke ranks and ran. The whole Yankee army just threw away their guns, abandoned a lot of their artillery, and fled. They passed senators and representatives in their rush to leave the battlefield. The women abandoned their picnics and rode in terror back toward Washington. We watched them go and laughed. I watched one of our troopers jump on a surrey and assist a terrified lady to turn away from the battlefield and back toward Washington. We were sure glad it wasn't us who lost the battle. If those reinforcements from West Virginia hadn't arrived in time, we might've lost, and the Yanks would have won the day.

I sat with my men that evening, reviewing what we'd done. It seemed like a nightmare; we lost Bill Runyon from Orange, and I'd seen when he had fallen, but he was facing the enemy. I turned him over and saw what a Minié ball had done to his chest. Now, of the four of us that had volunteered, there were three. The artillery had shot various types of shells at us; grape shot and canister were terrible and left large gaps in our lines. You could see the solid shot in flight; it would hit and bounce from the earth and stone and would mangle and mutilate whomever it hit.

I had taken part when we shot our first volley. I trained my rifle on the chest of an advancing trooper. "Fire," I screamed, and my gun joined others of my company. The man was lifted into the air and fell straight backward. His arms were thrown to each side of his body, and he never moved. I advanced by him and made the mistake of looking down at his upturned face. It was the face of a young man, his eyes set with a look of surprise, his mouth black from loading his own gun, and powder from his bullets had made a black ring around his open mouth. My stomach fluttered, and vomit came into my throat. I swallowed hard and looked into his sightless eyes. *Some mother will miss him!* I thought.

I remember Preacher Martin, from back home, preaching, "Thou shall not kill." Tears came into my eyes. The soldier was going to kill me if he could, I reasoned. I looked at my trembling hands. A young soldier, wearing the blue of the Northern army, no older than I, came here to fight for his belief, and I killed him.

"I'm just not cut out for this," I said to myself.

My squad had reloaded. I put the cartridge into my mouth and tore off the bullet; the powder I rammed into the barrel of my rifle, and the wad and Minie ball were forced down as well. I rammed them home and reached for the cap. I looked again at the advancing blue line. "Ready, aim, fire!" I cried, and another blue enemy fell. I had now killed two, but it wasn't as hard as the first one; I didn't look into his eyes. Our military chaplain had explained that when Moses brought the Ten Commandments down from the mountain, what the commandment "Thou shall not kill" meant was, "Thou shall not commit murder," and didn't apply to fighting as a soldier.

I saw many of the several thousand rifles that the Northern troops had discarded across the battlefield when they fled in terror. We captured twenty-six pieces of artillery, thirty-four caissons, and sets of harness, ten battery wagons, and a large number of wagons and ambulances. There were 460 dead federal army troops littering the fields, and 387 of our own brave men had also been slain in battle. We'd captured over thirteen hundred of the enemy. The stone bridge on the Warrenton Turnpike had been clogged by overturned wagons, and there were many abandoned wagons and surrey to the west of the bridge.

Our unit followed the enemy onto the Washington Turnpike, and it was there that we saw pots and kettles over fires with food cooking in them. Hanging in some of the trees were quarters of beef, and there were loaded wagons by the roadside. The wagons contained bread and provisions, as well as munitions in other wagons. We were a hungry group of soldiers, and we stopped to eat their cooked food.

I learned later that if we would've pursued their army, we might've taken Washington. Longstreet wanted a pursuit but was stopped by General Bonham. Longstreet was within cannon range of Centerville and wanted to fire on the retreating, demoralized federals. The federal army was very weary, for many of their troops marched forty miles that day and fought seven hours and retreated over the turnpike a ways east of Centerville before they were halted. If we had attacked them there, we might've played havoc with them, to cause their retreat to continue into Washington.

Our first battle was complete, and we were all weary but thankful that we'd survived our initial battle of the War between the States. I lay in my tent that evening, and in the middle of the night, I suddenly sat up. I was wet with perspiration, for I saw in my dreams the face of that young man that I had killed. I rose from my bed roll and took my canteen and poured cool water over my head. The battle was over, but that young man's death would cause many nightmares in years to come and would one day nearly kill me.

•

A week or two after the battle, my squad was detailed to act as pickets near the headquarters of General Joseph E. Johnson, the supreme commander of our army, near Manassas Junction. I stood at the door to our headquarters and checked all credentials of those wishing to enter the tent. General Beauregard presented himself with his staff, and of course, I permitted entrance. Just a few minutes later, General G. W. Smith and his staff arrived. These two generals were corps commanders under Johnson.

"Halt," I said as a civilian approached. "Advance and identify yourself!" I cried as two of my men stepped forward with fixed bayonets.

"I am Jefferson Davis, president of the Confederate States of America."

General Smith was at the door and stated, "It's all right, Sergeant. He is who he says he is."

I stood at stiff attention as I presented my very best salute.

As President Davis passed me, I could see the interior of the tent and the various officers surrounding a table covered with a map of Washington, D.C. I stood where I could hear what was going on, for I knew something very important was about to transpire. The entire group saluted the president, and then they got down to business.

"My congratulations are in order for the brilliant victory at Bull Run," said the president.

"Thank you, sir," Johnson replied.

"Now, let us discuss this new maneuver which you are proposing," continued the president.

"First, may I present our problem, sir," began General Johnson. "Since the fourth of August, the Federals have been reinforcing their forces in the Washington area. Our spies have seen an influx of approximately one hundred thousand new troops, composed of one hundred ten regiments and thirty batteries of artillery. They have excellent equipment and supplies, and, on the other hand, we have difficulty in clothing our troops and our supplies are scarce. If we sit here and watch the enemy grow in number and have better guns, clothing, food, and supplies, they'll have a much larger army for the next phase of this war," continued Johnson. "It is my idea, and it's supported by both General Beauregard and General Smith, that we attack Washington and disrupt this reinforcement situation," stated General Johnson.

"How many troops would that take?" asked President Davis.

"General Beauregard and I have set the need at sixty thousand troops. These should be seasoned troops, and not new recruits. General Smith believes that it can be done with fifty thousand troops. Our army here now numbers about forty thousand."

"So, you need an additional twenty thousand troops; they should be seasoned troops and well-supplied," said the president as he shook his head. "If we take our experienced troops away from various areas, it'll weaken those areas and make them prime targets for our enemy to attack. I don't agree that thinning our ranks of these troops to attack Washington is the thing to do at this time," said President Davis, and that was the end of that.

The meeting was over and the group continued with small talk. The president came through the tent door and looked right at me. My salute was answered smartly by his.

"Sergeant, I wish I had twenty thousand more troops like you. You've a military background, don't you? What is your name?" he asked.

"I am Sergeant Tom McDowell of Company A of the 7th Virginia Infantry, Kemper's brigade. I attended Virginia Military Institute, sir."

"Colonel Kemper's brigade, eh? Virginia Military Institute is well-known and has loaned us a great professor who we must from now on call 'Stonewall' Jackson for his stand at Bull Run," said Davis with a smile.

"Yes, sir," I said, and he was gone.

I had witnessed and overheard a conference that could have changed the outcome of the war.

THE HISTORY OF
KEMPER'S BRIGADE

Our history of Company A of the Seventh Virginia Infantry, Kemper's Brigade and Pickett's Division, First Army Corps, is well-known. Our history, of course, is my history, for I didn't miss a day in four years fighting alongside my men and those volunteers who came from Orange and Madison all the way back in 1861. Of the four who signed up in Orange and became a part of the volunteer group, only I survived. The war was long, and the battles were bloody and severe.

Bill Runyon was killed at Bull Run. Bill Deane, who was concerned that he wouldn't stand before a bayonet charge, fought through many such charges, but was killed by grape shot, which were leaded shots the size of grapes fired from cannon, following General William Taliaferro in the Pickett charge at Gettysburg. Taliaferro captured Lt. Alonzo Cushing's Battery A 4th US Artillery just prior to being mortally wounded by enemy infantry. General Garnett had also been killed and General Kemper was seriously wounded, and we thought he'd lost his life, but he fell into the hands of the Union army and was taken to a field hospital. He was imprisoned for three months, and in an exchange of prisoners, he was traded for the Northern, General Graham. Kemper's wounds were so serious that he could not resume command of active forces.

Ralph Smith from Orange was also killed in the charge at Gettysburg, leaving only me to survive our group. I lost some good, loving, and caring friends in those first months, and felt so much alone that I failed to make many friends during the rest of the war. Company A had a very good history, taking part in the First Battle of Manassas, Williamsburg, Malvern Hill, South Mountain, Sharpsburg, Fredericksburg, Gettysburg, the Suffolk and North Carolina campaigns, as well as the battles of Plymouth, Cold Harbor, and many months in the battle of Petersburg. Our company was considered one of the top outfits, and we gave more punishment than we received.

At Gettysburg, in the famous Pickett Charge, our division lost seventy percent of its force. Four generals were killed, and General James L. Kemper was seriously wounded. Most of the senior officers were killed. It was after Gettysburg that I received a huge promotion to major. Indeed, I was proud of the achievement, but my heart ached over my lost comrades. The division that had once been so full of life, had declined to the point that General George Pickett complained to General Lee that his command "was no more." What was left of the division was pulled out of line and held in readiness, in the event the Northern troops would surge forward over the dead bodies of the 7th Infantry Division. The division lay there, the gray and butternut uniformed troops, shot to pieces and bloating in the heat. They'd been ordered forward and died out in the open fields, all facing the enemy. The enemy artillery fire had been most destructive and was composed mainly of canister and grape shot. The timers had been set to explode near, or just above, our advancing troops. Infantry volleys of musket fire from the enemy had mowed huge gaps though our lines. As one line fell, another line advanced. After we were pulled back, I lay in the grass and took a count of who was left. My trousers were shot full of holes; my canteen had a large hole through it. I was very shaken and dazed that I'd survived when so many brave men had fallen.

"Thank you, Lord, for getting me through this!" I cried. "Oh, God, where is my command, my friends?"

They were lying dead in the fields. I found myself trying to remember where I'd last seen this one or that. They now all looked the same, like gray logs or bundles of hay lying in the fields, waiting to be gathered for harvest. Some bodies were bloated from the hot sun. It was an exceedingly hot day; so much so that the fields were dancing before my eyes. The fields were full of wounded calling for water; some were rolling in agony on the ground, but many were only trunks of what used to be men. Slaughter! Terrible! I wanted to get up and run away from it all, but I felt a sense of honor to stay and hold fast.

I heard myself, but I seemed so far away, calling my troops to hold a line. I cast aside my canteen and took one from a fallen soldier who'd been killed so long ago that rigor mortis had set in. I had to lift his stiff body and maneuver the canteen in various ways to clear it from his body. The water was very warm, and there was a faint smell of death still on the canteen. I poured the water out and called to a young soldier who was bringing in water to refresh our troops to fill my canteen.

•

It was around March of 1862 that the Union army's General McClellan landed at Yorktown and began what was known as the Peninsula Campaign. This was our next encounter as a part of Johnson's army after Bull Run, and we were with General Longstreet. We were holding the Yankees, trying to keep them from advancing too fast until a strong army of troops could be in place to stop their advance on Richmond. Our stand at Williamsburg bloodied McClellan, and our division was in the very middle of the fighting. My squad did so well that Colonel Kemper promoted me in the field to second lieutenant.

I was promoted to first lieutenant at South Mountain, when our brigade only numbered about eight hundred men, and we met the Union Commander Edward Hatch with three thousand five hundred men. We fought them to a standstill, and in his report to Federal General Hooker, Hatch stated he was engaged by a force of four to five thousand men. I was promoted to captain at the bloody battle of Sharpsburg; then, with all the loss in officers at Gettysburg, I was moved up to replace one of the positions left vacant by the hundred percent loss of our majors in the division. There was just no one else to fill the position within our ranks. My brief schooling at Virginia Military Institute was mainly responsible for my quick promotions. I also had conducted myself as a very able officer.

The responsibility of my new position matured me into an officer who cared for his troops. I insisted that, even while we were in resting areas, training be continued. Since we still fought by squads, I taught the men and their officers under my command how to pivot in angles and to maneuver to each command. I also insisted that my men be led and not driven. I wanted my officers leading the squad rather that standing behind it with drawn swords to force them forward.

APPOMATTOX COURT HOUSE

We'd been dug in at Petersburg, and I'd found trench warfare to be a horrible, dirty way to fight. A man had to keep his head down, or some Yankee blue belly sharpshooter would end his life. Body lice and fleas were rampant. We all stank and were filthy dirty. We were so close to the enemy that we called to one another. Some troops became well acquainted and cussed at, as well as kidded with, one another.

"Hey, Johnny, can you smell that bacon frying? I hear that you ain't eating too well," called a Northern soldier from a few yards away.

"Okay, Blue Belly, can you tell me why you call us Johnnies?" asked a Confederate soldier.

"The way I heard it, there were two talking, and our sentry said that you guys just reminded him of Johnny Bulls. So, you are nothing but Johnnies."

The British were called Johnny Bulls, and some still lived to remember the War of 1812. A torrent of vile profanity came from the Confederate trenches.

I got very little exercise living in the trenches, and the food was atrocious. Our troops were surrounded and under siege, our supplies were gone, and food now consisted of some parched corn that our foragers had found for us. I shared my corn with the mare I had taken from home during the Wilderness campaign. I kept her in an abandoned building with other officer's mounts. It was April of 1865, and the handwriting was plain for us to see. The war was lost and we'd soon be forced to capitulate. All knew it to be a fact, but we'd fought so long and so hard that some of us couldn't even think of surrendering.

The Yanks ruptured our lines and invaded some of our trenches to the point that, unless we retreated, all would come to an end. General Lee had assembled thirty thousand of his remaining troops, and the order was for a surprise breakout through the fortifications that surrounded us. Would it be possible for the grey fox to slip away from the Union army into some naturally defendable area to regroup and to carry on?

On April 2, 1865, Lee sent dispatches of his intentions to Richmond, and to his scattered forces north of the James River, for his troops to join him. The troops in the trenches were told to keep quiet as they slipped through enemy lines. There was a tremendous explosion as the magazines of Fort Drewry were blown up. Also, to the north, the sky had a dull, red glow; Richmond was on fire, and about one third of the city would burn that night.

When the retreating appeared to be successful, the explosion at the fort, as well as the burning of the city, brought to the attention of the Union army the moving of the Confederates. On the third of April, the mayor of Richmond surrendered the city, and Grant moved forward with his army of approximately eighty thousand men, led by Sheridan's cavalry, to try to cut off our forces and to seal up the breach in his lines.

We'd heard that there were supplies awaiting us at Amelia Court House to the West. We were weak with hunger and needed rest and a good meal. Some of the older men had to be carried. By the time the army got to Amelia Court House, the train that was supposed to deliver the supplies wasn't there. It'd been sent on into Richmond and was now captured by Grant's army. Our men fell out along the way. Some wept from disappointment, and it was a severe blow to General Lee. Some stupid railroad employee had thrust the dart of hunger and disappointment into the heart of the Confederate army, by sending our supplies on to Richmond, instead of leaving them at Amelia Court House.

At Sailor's Creek, the pursuing Northern army caught up with our troops and about ten thousand of Ewell's rear guard were surrounded and captured along with some of our artillery and wagons.

Along the way, some regular supplies had been received, and the army paused at Farmville to permit the troops to cook and prepare the food. They had received two day's rations. Troops were now deserting in droves, and the effective army of Northern Virginia was reduced to about ten thousand men. General Gordon led an attack against the Union army in an attempt to break through to Appomattox for more supplies. The attack was blunted, and now our army was at the mercy of the much larger Northern force. Lee corresponded repeatedly with General Grant, and terms were given for his surrender.

Three things were of extreme importance and of benefit to me. The train loaded with our supplies was brought back from Richmond, and we cooked and ate until we were full again. All the officers could keep their side arms, and the men could keep their horses. Back when my final promotion went through and we were holding our lines and awaiting Grant at the Wilderness, I had caught a ride to Orange on an ambulance, and Dad let me bring my blue grulla, Jane, back with me. The Confederate army did not supply their officers with horses.

Upon the signing of the surrender, and within three days, thousands of soldiers were set free and pardoned. Many hadn't a cent in their pockets and were far from home. I was very fortunate that Appomattox was only about seventy miles southwest of home. I took my time and was home in three days. During that time, I ate very little food, but everyone was in the same boat. I was no longer saluted or fed as an officer. We still tried to care for one another, and I must say that the "blue bellies" did care for our wounded.

HOMECOMING ISN'T WHAT
I THOUGHT IT'D BE

As I rode up our lane on April 12, 1865, it had been four years since I left home.

I saw that the ground hadn't been plowed and last year's corn was still in the field. Weeds were everywhere and growing along the fence rows that bordered the lane. The slaves appeared to be at home, for there was smoke coming from cooking stoves in their kitchens.

Three black children were playing in one yard, but who'd that be? I slowed my horse to get a better look at them. *Let's see, the kids are four years older than when I'd last seen them. But who are they? Whose child is that?* I thought. I put my spur to my horse slightly and quickened its pace.

The main house looked shabby and run down. Grass needed mowing, and the garden was full of last year's weeds. *What in the world?* I wondered. *Oh, God! What has happened? No sign of life! Surely the Williamses had seen me coming up the lane.* I tied my horse to the iron figure at the edge of the porch and dismounted. Weariness, which had been gnawing at me for the past two hours, vanished as I stared at my home. Still, no one came to the door, nor was there any sound. As I walked onto the porch, a pigeon flew from its nest above one of the columns that supported the ceiling over the porch. *Where was Shep, our dog?*

I tried the front door, but found it to be locked. Walking to the large front window, I looked through a filthy glass into a ransacked room. By now, alarm had really set in, and I was becoming frantic. Where was Dad? And where was the Williams family? Those people living in our slave houses, along the entrance, just who were they? I didn't know them, nor did I see a familiar face. Leaving my horse tied at the front gate, I walked back down the lane and approached the first dwelling. A middle-aged black woman came to the door.

"Who're you?" she questioned.

"I'm Tom McDowell. Where are the Williams?"

"Mr. McDowell, he dead, and the Williams, they moved to a house in town."

"Dead?" I heard my voice almost whisper the word. "My dad is dead? When? Why didn't someone get in touch with me?"

"Sir, I is sorry, but Mr. McDowell, he died over a year ago from some kind of sickness, they said. No one seemed to know where you is. The Williams, they tried to find you and mailed letters, but got no answers."

"Who are you, and where are our field hands that lived here when I left four years ago?" I asked.

"All da hands was freed cord'n to Mr. McDowell's will, and people come and took dey houses and sold dem. We be free, and we be rent'n dem from the county as taxes due on ever un of dem. We been hav'n trouble with some mean boys in the area, and three weeks ago, dey broken en de house and tore up a lot of yo stuff. Yo daddy was buried in the family plot nex yr momma. We is sorry that you had to come home to dis."

I hurried to our family cemetery. I knelt at the graves of my mother and father and wept sorely. He now had his wish to be with her. I remembered his consumption and his terrible cough. I didn't want to break into the house, so I made camp in the front yard and spent another night under the stars. I was so troubled that I slept little.

•

The next morning, I was at our family's lawyer, full of questions about what had happened while I was away. I learned that Dad had many debts that went back several years. Taxes due on the place had to be paid, and the county, after awaiting a year, had called for certain portions of the property to be sold. Aunt Goldie had written to me, but her letters had come back. Our division had moved around so often, and was in battle so much, that the letters had not caught up. My lawyer suggested that I sell the place; I'd no slaves to work the land. The equipment, plow, harrow, riding horse planter, rake, and various other tools had been sold at auction. The lawyer handed me an envelope with fifty dollars of greenbacks in it.

"After paying your debts and taxes," my lawyer explained, "I've withheld my retainer, and that is the balance. Your slave houses, cattle, and horses all came to three thousand dollars. The ledger sheets will show the totals after all bills were paid. This leaves the main house and land now free and clear. In case you're interested, I've a buyer who wishes you to consider his offer. You'll find his proposition, with earnest money, in this envelope. All you need to do is sign the contract, and you'll be paid in greenbacks. I feel that the offer is fair, especially now that your dad is gone."

Prior to leaving the lawyer's office, I obtained the address of Aunt Goldie and Uncle Buck. I walked from his office with head down, wishing to see a friendly face. All seemed to be strangers. I needed to find Aunt Goldie and Uncle Buck, as I needed someone who understood just how low I was. I stopped at the street corner and opened the envelope to look at the offer: seventeen hundred acres at twenty-five dollars an acre, to be paid in greenbacks, and a balance due at settlement of forty-two thousand five hundred dollars. There was an earnest payment made out in a certified check in the amount of one hundred dollars that would be redeemed at closing.

I stood there, shocked, and realized I hadn't eaten in three days. The fifty in greenbacks would pay for many meals to come, and I needed some clothes. I had outgrown my wardrobe, which I had left behind when I joined the service.

•

Aunt Goldie and Uncle Buck were glad to see me. They told me of finding Dad when he had the spell, and that he didn't linger, but died quickly. The Williams had tried to find me, but couldn't. The funeral had been held at the house and they told what they'd done by preparing his body for burial and putting him in a pine box. They'd no money for the funeral, nor enough to change the wording on Mom's tombstone to include Dad. I told them I understood. I gave them money from my fifty dollars to repay what they'd spent. They'd used money kept at the house for household expenses, but had to use some of their own too.

"How do you like being free now? I knew Dad had your emancipation in his will and I'm happy for you," I said.

"Things were horribly bad at first. We tried to hire out as house servants, but didn't know what to charge, and we had to rent ourselves a house. We got no work until we found what others was gettin' fo their work, and we started askin' fo 'bout the same. Tom, things has been very hard, and there was times that we didn't have enough to eat. We put out a garden last year and used some of the seed we had left over from plantin' at your place. We hope you don't mind. What you gonna do, Tom? We'll work for you and not charge you but little if you'll help us with our expenses," said Aunt Goldie with a look of hope in her eyes.

"Thanks, but I'm not sure just what I'll do. I've always wanted to see California, and if I sell the farm, I'll be free to see the West. I've been reading a few of those dime cowboy books, and it has really got me to thinking of my future. I know that the books are about half true, but there's something appealing to them," I answered.

"Tom, I guess you know that Audrey Jefferson is married, and that Wilma Caroline is married with three children all in the four years that you've been gone," Aunt Goldie added.

"I don't care too much about Wilma, but that Audrey, who did she marry?" I inquired.

"She married one of Harry Dizney's boys. The middle one, I believe," said Aunt Goldie, as my heart sank.

" I'd plans when I got out of service to court her."

"No use in stayn' around here now. I'm twenty-five and back home, and all the girls I went to school with are married. Times are really so different, and Dad being gone wasn't what I expected. By the way, where's the key to the house?" I asked.

A feeling of despair settled over me and my heart ached. I felt lonely and in need of someone to love me and give me comfort. Aunt Goldie was sympathetic and hugged me in her loving way.

"Tom, there's a brick under the front step on the right side. I put the key there," said Aunt Goldie.

•

The next morning, I arrived early at the lawyer's office.

"Is Mr. Crawford in?" I asked the girl in his front office.

"I believe that I heard him come in the back door. Just a minute and I'll see," was her reply. I met Mr. Crawford in the front office.

"Good to see you, Tom," said Mr. Crawford, extending his hand. "Have you come with the idea of selling your farm? I thought you might take a few days to think it over and ask advice from some of your dad's friends. I truly believe that the offer was a good one and we can close it in about a month."

"Yes, sir, I am interested. A month seems a long time, though. Can't we close more quickly? I'm making plans to head west. My close friends were all killed in the war, and I'm at a loss in what to do with myself," I explained.

"Tom, it'll take a month. There's too much work in searching that title. I'm not sure that my client will be ready to close any sooner than that. And Tom, I can't represent both the buyer and the seller; since he has paid me a retainer, you'll need to get a lawyer. Young William Dizney is married now and has some experience in title work. He'd do fine, if you want to consider him," said Mr. Crawford.

"Thanks. You'll find a signed contract for that sale in the envelope, and I'd like your secretary to notarize it for me," I said as I walked into the outer office with the papers.

Soon, the transaction was completed. With that, I walked out the door and down to a clothing store that I'd known of before my military service began.

"Hello, Mr. Willougher. I see you're still in business. It's good to see that some things haven't changed. I want to see some clothing and I need everything: several pair of underwear, shirts, a jacket, and a broadcloth suit," I said.

"Welcome home, Tom. Sure good to see you. I heard you were home and you look great. I hear your outfit really had it hard. So many good boys are gone; I believe we've lost about twenty from Orange. Might be a few more or less, but most were your age. Saw Tim Wilson yesterday and he looked terrible; he'd lost an arm, and it's not fully healed yet. Mrs. Wilson will get him well, but it'll take some time. Northern troops will be coming into town soon, but I hope not to bully us. Tom, come this way and let me measure you," said Mr. Willougher, ushering me in front of a mirror.

"You've filled out, my boy! A forty-six expanded chest and thirty-four-inch waist. The army made a man out of you," he continued.

Toting several bundles, I made for the door, and as I went into the street, I felt the worst four years of my young life were behind me. It'd take me a long time to get over the idea that I was back home and out of harm's way. I stayed in the big house by myself, though Aunt Goldie came over often to make sure I was eating well. At night, I dreamed and relived a part of the war, and would wake to hear the crickets outside my window. Where was I? Are the pickets alert? Did I hear the rebel cry? Was that a shot?

•

Aunt Goldie was paid out of the balance of what I had left. I planned to give Goldie and Buck fifteen hundred dollars of the sales price of the farm to help them get along. That was more than they'd earn in the next five years, at least. While waiting for the real estate closing, I made several plans regarding my trip to California. At first, I thought I'd travel by train to New Orleans and take a schooner and sail around South America and on to Los Angeles. As I considered the freight costs, my passage, my horse, and my pack mule, I began to get second thoughts. Besides, I was in no hurry, and I wanted to see as much of the country as possible, so I changed my plans and decided to go south to Texas and try to keep away from the snowy areas. I could take my horse and buy either a buggy or a couple of mules to carry my supplies.

Aunt Goldie was a wonderful cook, so I ate well and began to put on weight. I remembered to do my exercises, for vigorous training was a real part of my life. The good food, exercising, riding, and running put me in tip-top shape. I fed my horse well with corn, oats, and some good hay. The two mules and my mare had new saddles and bridles, as well as pack saddles. I had Mom's tombstone engraved to include Dad's name. They were together now. It was something he'd long hoped for. The cemetery wasn't included in the sale, and was deeded into my name.

The closing was set for eight o'clock in the morning, and the buyer was on time. The money had been deposited into an account set up for me at the local bank. I wrote checks and filled my purse with greenbacks for future expenses. The buyer was from Philadelphia and was tired of city life. He thought he could get a good deal due to the war's winding down, and buying early, he could get what he wanted. When the deed was recorded, I took a check from my new account over to Goldie and Buck. They wept and laughed and wept again and declared themselves the richest black folks in Virginia. Then we all wept as I said good-bye to them and started west to a new life away from war and blood. I went seeking adventure, to find my fortune and perhaps companionship. It was the eighth day of June 1865 as I rode down the road toward the town of Gordonsville; Longstreet's old camping ground. I was on my way! I'd turned a new page in my life, and was hoping that many of the storms of life over the last four years could be put into the past.

JOURNEY WEST

I journeyed southwest and crossed the Appalachian Mountains into Tennessee. The roads were filled with soldiers on their way home from the war. At Memphis, I took a ferry across the Mississippi into Arkansas and then into Texas at Texarkanna. My trip took me through Dallas and Fort Worth and then on to Abilene. I estimated the mileage to be twelve hundred fifty miles, and I averaged forty miles a day and arrived in Abilene, Texas, on the 19th day of July, 1865.

I'd been in Texas for two weeks. The area was a rolling plain and the Texans were friendly. Most of the Confederate soldiers had returned home, and I'd shared some food with them along my way. Many were walking on sore feet, and I'd invited them to share my campfire, as well as whatever else I had. On more than one occasion, I'd shifted the loads on my pack animals and carried a returning soldier to his home. Some had been held in captivity, having been imprisoned in the last stages of the war, and were hurting and unhealthy. Their uniforms were moth-eaten, dirty, and smelly. I loaned my extra razor and several bars of soap, as well as clean clothing, which I knew they'd never return. All were most anxious to get home. We'd sit at night around a fire and relive some exploits, which we'd share. These were my kind of men, and I enjoyed their war stories and companionship. We parted at their homes, and declared we'd not forget one another. Most were received back home with great joy and with screams of delight.

My knowledge of the state of Texas was broadened when I carried a returning college professor westward toward Austin. He told me that Texas was established as a republic in October 1836, and had formed a constitution modeled on the US Constitution. With General Houston as their new president, Texans enjoyed eight years of independence before applying to be annexed to the United States. Many in the Northern part of the United States were against the annexation of a slave state; President Van Buren was one of them and the project was put on hold until the next election. General Harrison was elected president, but lived such a short time that his vice president, Tyler, on the death of Harrison, became the new president.

President Tyler was a Virginian and was extremely interested in the annexation. I brought this bit of history into our conversation, as I reminded the professor that we Virginians got them into a good thing.

The professor told me, "I'm not so sure that you all did us any favors. Here I am hungry, naked, dirty, and have a bad taste in my mouth. We got whipped, and that taste will be in my mouth for a long time. They didn't treat me too well in that prison camp. I hope that I never see some of those guards down here, for I'll kill them if I can."

He used profanity in his description of his captors.

Companionship that I'd found among my fellow troopers and companions in the Kemper Brigade was experienced anew about my campfire.

I saw veterans with peg legs, some without arms, and not fully recovered from their wounds. Many of the returning wounded had been dismissed from a Union hospital to go home to die.

They were careful not to complain, but wondered how they'd be received at home, or how they could make a living in their poor physical condition. Often, my thoughts would turn to that first soldier that I'd killed and how his parents might be waiting for him to walk in their door.

I AM ROBBED

I had turned more to the northwest and was near the panhandle of Texas. It was one evening, right at twilight, when I stopped early to make camp. I'd found an excellent campsite near a stream that was running fresh and clear. I cut up a few potatoes and cut some bacon from a pork belly. The sun still gave off a red glow in the west, and a whippoorwill was calling to his mate from a wooded area just to the north. I was now more cautious regarding my surroundings, as I was in Indian country. I was trying to be careful, as I'd heard news of marauding bands of Indians, and whenever I heard a bird call, I paid strict attention. My fire was putting out a thin line of smoke that was bothering me. The pine wood was wet and no other type of wood was near at hand. I needed dry wood, so there would be less smoke. Along the trail came a lone rider, and I could hear him almost a hundred yards before he reached my camp.

"Hello. May I come in?" he called out.

His voice was just loud enough to reach me, and I understood that he didn't want to attract undue attention.

"Come on in and sit," I replied. "There's bacon and hot coffee, and I plan to fry a potato."

I'd put my rifle against a nearby pine tree, and it was out of sight from my visitor.

"Thanks. I believe I will," he remarked.

He dismounted from a very weary horse that appeared to be going lame. The poor animal was blowing and its tongue was hanging from its mouth. I hated to see any animal abused, and studied the poor, lathered creature.

"I've an old towel there. You want to rub him down and walk

him some to cool him off, I—" I stopped suddenly, for my visitor stood there smiling at me, having drawn a pistol, and was pointing the weapon at me.

"I'm going to eat your food, drink your water, and steal your horse. I'm sorry that I can't stay, for I'm in a hurry, you see. Let me tell you this: if you as much as move toward that pistol, I'll shoot you dead! You understand? I've got a posse about five miles back, and they've been crowding me. That mare of yours may well make the difference," he growled.

I studied his bearded face. His bloodshot eyes had no smile, and he seemed like a hunted animal. He appeared to be a half breed and had a scar on his left cheek. His clothes were matted with perspiration and dust.

"Mister," I said, "be good to my horse." I pointed my thumb toward my mare. "She's my old friend and was with me the last year of the war," I pleaded.

"Buddy, put your saddle on her for me while I eat this bacon," he ordered.

He gulped down the hot coffee, and took a fork and lifted a half-done piece of bacon from the pan and rolled it around in his mouth to cool it. He mounted my mare and noticed the rifle boot was empty.

"Where's the rifle?" he yelled angrily, and turned his revolver toward me. Before I could answer, he turned his head to one side in a listening posture, spurred my mare, and rode through the trees toward the trail.

"There he goes!" came a cry from half a dozen riders.

They spurred their horses past me in hot pursuit. I ran for my rifle and paused to check it. The trail consisted of a group of small hills, and there was just enough light to see parts of the trail in the last light of the closing day. Down the trail, the tops of two hills were highlighted by the sun. I estimated the second hill to be a distance of three hundred yards. I set the sights as I'd often done in battle. I sat on the ground with the rifle snug against my shoulder and waited for the rider to reach the lighted area of the second hill. I saw his checkered shirt and a lump came into my throat as I considered the chance of hitting my mare. The rifle steadied as I squeezed the trigger. The recoil came, and the flame shot from the barrel. I looked ahead and the rider was gone from sight.

Now what in the world would I do? No horse, except that poor, trembling animal that stood with lowered head. I turned my attention to the creature and found in my pack an old piece of cloth. I rubbed the horse down and talked to it as I fastened a feeding bag over his head that was full of oats. I'd just taken the skillet off the fire when I heard horses coming back down the trail. The posse was returning.

"Hello, the camp!" one cried.

They came in leading my mare, and I was so happy to see her.

"That was really a great shot, mister. You shot him right off the horse. Where were you when you shot?" one inquired.

Across the mare laid the man, blood oozing from a gaping wound in his left shoulder, and his eyes were angry and full of pain.

"I'm Ranger Matt Willard from Big Spring, and we've been running Juan Garcia for two days now. He escaped from jail after we caught him a few weeks back. There's a bounty on his head of a thousand dollars, which I'd say belongs to you. I guess you did the shooting, as you're the only other person we've seen. Show us where you were when you shot him. Sam, have you got any more pieces of cloth to bind him up a little better. He's bleeding all down his shirt in the back. Lay him on the ground there while we go see where this guy was when he shot. This is it for tonight. Do you mind if we share your camp?" asked the ranger.

"I'm Thomas McDowell from Virginia and I'm just passing through this beautiful state. Ranger, I'd certainly be most happy to have you share my camp. I've some bacon, and I'd started to peel a potato or two. I've beans in those cans, and there are some biscuits, which I made this morning in that camp oven. If one of you men would build up that fire and start frying more bacon, it won't be long and we can eat. I've extra coffee in that tin," I said.

Little interest was displayed in the evening meal, as the posse and the ranger just wanted to know where I'd been when I made that long shot. The ranger shook his head as he looked up the trail.

There was just barely enough light left to see the top of the second hill.

"I guess we were under the first hill when you shot?" he inquired. "Where in the world did you ever learn to shoot like that? Bet you were a sharpshooter in the army," he drawled. "That must have been at least three hundred yards."

"Learned to shoot when I was a boy and it carried over into my college days. In the army, I taught soldiers the use of the rifle versus the bored barrel that wasn't rifled. The bullet that came from a rifled barrel went from the barrel in a spiraling manner and was more accurate. This gun of mine, I bought near Houston when I passed through."

"What army were you in, Tom?" inquired the ranger, with hesitation.

"I was a major in Company A of the 7th Infantry, Kemper's brigade, Pickett's Division, First Army Corps," I replied.

"You were in the charge at Gettysburg?" asked one of the posse.

"Yes," I said.

"Most of us were in Hood's Texans and in Longstreet's division" said the Ranger. "I was in the 8th Texas cavalry."

"I was sure glad to see Hood's Texans at the battle of the Wilderness when General Lee stood along the road and greeted you, pointing where he wanted you in the line," I said. "You double-timed by the general, calling, 'To the rear, Lee. To the rear!' I was there; I saw, and heard, and was mighty proud of you that day," I said. "The 8th Texas Cavalry, wasn't that Terry's Rangers?"

"Yes, we were called that along with Wharton's regiment and some other names that a Sunday school teacher wouldn't repeat," smiled the ranger.

Another member of the posse that had been in Hood's Texans spoke up.

"Thanks, Tom. We'd marched all night, all the way from Gordonsville and we were late; we were supposed to attack over the guys in the trenches. As you remember, Burnside's troops were about to overrun our guys, and we got there just in time."

"You guys sure looked good coming up that road," I answered.

Supper was prepared and horses fed and hobbled where they'd get good grass. The wound of the bandit was dressed again and his handcuffs put back in place. He sat watching every move that I made and there was a look of hatred and anger on his scarred face.

We ate our evening meal and bedded down for the night. The posse and I got along just fine, and morning came too soon for most of us. We all were tired, but happy. Breakfast was a shared meal.

"You think Garcia can travel?" asked one of the posse, pointing to the robber.

"He sure looks done in. I've got to get back to my store," stated another.

"Tom, you can ride back with us if you like, for you've that reward coming. I'll have to wire to Austin for it, but I believe it may take a couple weeks before I can get it. We've a good hotel and restaurant where you can spend some time. If you don't have the cash for lodging, you can sleep at the jail," stated the ranger.

"Tom, a lot of cow hands that ride the grub trail stay at my livery barn. This time of the year, they all have work, but you're welcome to put your horse and sleep there if you want," said another.

"Ranger, who gets Garcia's horse? Is it state property?" asked another, looking toward the robber's animal.

"It very well could be stolen property. That killer didn't break out of the jail by himself. He was aided, but I've no idea whose horse that is. If it isn't claimed in a week or so it could be Tom's. It may go to my office to help us with our expenses," said the ranger.

The camp was about ready to move. Horses were all saddled and gear was loaded on the mules. Dishes had been taken to the nearby creek, where they were washed and sanded dry.

"I sure would hate to feed you guys on a daily schedule. I can tell you were confederates; hollow clear to the toes," I chided.

They all agreed, but blamed each other for eating more than any other person in Hood's army. I had my camp near to Sulphur Springs, which was about thirty miles from Big Spring where the ranger had his office. All of us felt sorry for our wounded prisoner. He had sustained such a gaping, ugly wound in his left shoulder and must have been very painful. We had nothing to deaden his pain.

The robber complained very little about his wound, but we only slowed enough to make sure he'd be alive and ready for trial when the judge came into the area.

•

Big Spring was a cowboys' paradise. There were the usual buildings with the false fronts. There was a bank, post office, three saloons, a livery stable, a mercantile store, a jail, a barber shop, a restaurant, and a hotel. I liked what I saw, for it was much like my own home town of Orange. I quickly became a celebrity as the posse told of my shooting the bandit and of his capture.

"You looking for a job?" asked the mayor of the town. "We could use a good town marshal. You could work well with Ranger Willard. Matt needs a good ranger, so maybe you could do both jobs and the payroll would keep you here. We need help with the Indians. You think about it, hear?"

Ranger Willard went to the telegraph office to wire for the reward, and then came over to the livery stable where I was tending to my horses and the prisoner's horse. The animal looked much better, and it appeared he'd recover completely from the abuse he'd suffered. I fed him oats and corn, and had the liveryman throw good, quality hay to all the animals. Well-satisfied with the care of my horses, I went to the hotel, where I registered and was pleasantly pleased with my room. I looked forward to sleeping in a bed, as it'd been over a month since I had. I opened my door on the way to the restaurant, and there was the ranger, trying to find my room number.

SUPPER WITH RANGER MATT AND FAMILY

"Tom, I've been home and reported what you did, and my wife Bess insisted that I just run over here and invite you to our home for supper. Supper'll be at six, and we live right down the street, just east of the mercantile store," the ranger drawled.

"Thanks, Matt. It has been over a month since I've eaten anyone's cooking but my own. I need a bath and my hair washed and cut. I could use a shave too. I'll try to get rid of a month on the trail, plus my beard. I'm looking forward to meeting your family," I said.

The hotel provided a big brass tub, and there were gallons of hot water brought for the bath.

After I'd soaked in the sudsy water and went through two cycles of soap and rinsing, I realized what I'd been missing by being out on the trail. I lay back in the barber's chair as he trimmed my long hair and shaved me with a sharp, straight razor. With a clean checkered shirt, black trousers, and a blue scarf (this was Texas' style) around my neck, I looked into the mirror, which hung in my room. I saw a rather handsome curly, black-haired, smiling, clean-shaven, even-toothed, young Romeo. As I thought of Romeo, I almost burst out laughing, for I hadn't had a girlfriend since I'd secretly admired Audrey before I'd gone off to war. I regretted losing her, so I might as well not even think of her. The barber had drenched my head with some sort of sweet-smelling hair tonic, which was still running down the side of my head. I took a towel and briskly cleaned my head and re-combed my hair.

The ranger's house was easily found and was neat in appearance. The house was frame with double-hung windows and clapboard siding. It gave an inviting appearance with a lamp light in a window. There was a porch all along the front of the dwelling. I tied my horse to an iron ring near the front gate of the picket fence. The ranger met me carrying an oil lamp and held the door while I entered.

"Welcome, Tom," he drawled. "Come on in."

"Did I hear someone?" asked a middle-aged blond lady. "Oh, good," she said as she saw me.

I towered a foot over her and I stood looking down into her upturned, smiling face. I'd taken my hat off as I entered the room.

"I'm Bess," she said, extending her hand. "I've heard so much about you that I feel I know you already."

I lightly shook her small hand.

"Pleased to meet you," was my response.

The folk around Orange, Virginia were descendents from Scotland, and I'd acquired, unknowingly, a southern scotch brogue accent. I turned toward the ranger, who took my hat, and as I turned back, I caught Bess studying me.

"Dinner will be ready and we'll eat as soon as Delight gets home. Delight is our only child. She teaches school in the winter months and works at the bank through the summer. She's a little late tonight," Bess informed me.

It was a warm evening and Bess had prepared some lemonade, which she offered Matt and me as we waited.

"I don't believe that I've heard of a girl called Delight," I said, just to make conversation.

"Matt named her for when he looked at her for the first time; the baby smiled and her deep dimple was a delight to him, he said," stated Bess. "I think I hear her now."

I saw a very pretty girl come sweeping through the front door and she stopped in the front parlor. It was evident that she hadn't expected anyone other than family to be at home. My being there completely captivated her, for she stood there for what seemed a half minute to study me. She sure had my full attention! She was a blond (her mother's hair) and had very green eyes. Her lips were generous and full and there was a deep dimple in her right cheek. She had an hourglass figure.

"Oh my land," I whispered, and hoped she hadn't heard me.

I realized that she was staring back, and we became aware of our interest in one another. She blushed a deep red. I feared I'd been rude.

"Delight, this is Tom McDowell from Virginia. I'm sure that the customers at the bank have been talking about him shooting that robber off his horse."

Delight extended her hand.

"How do you do?" she said shyly.

Her mother had come into the room and stood smiling.

"Honey, wash up, for we're ready to eat," she said.

Delight quickly vanished as the others made their way into the kitchen.

"I'll have water, Mother," Delight called from off the kitchen.

I suppose the family sat at their usual places; Matt faced his wife and I was seated across from Delight.

After a fine meal of country-fried chicken, potatoes, green beans, and then apple pie and coffee, we sat for a brief time around the table and talked. I tried not to stare at Delight, but I still caught her eye occasionally. Her light complexion really accented her blushing. I told of my military background and that I had reached a major in my division, and of my return home to find my dad dead. My wanting to see the United States, especially California, caught the interest of the entire family.

"A lot of our young men have been away in the service and are just now coming back," said Matt. "They have so far to get home, Tom," Matt changed the subject. "I hope that you're not completely set on that trip to California right now. Our mayor has approached me to see if you'd be interested in staying in this part of the country. We need a town marshal, and I could use some help in this reconstruction period. I'm not sure just what our ranger status will be. There's been a lot of talk that since we seceded from the Union, we're outside of the constitution of the United States, and should be considered as enemies and aliens of our country."

"Dad," said Delight. "I've read newspapers that have refuted such thinking and that President Abraham Lincoln had a more generous plan for we rebel states. In his second inaugural address, he said, let me see if I can remember some of it: 'With malice toward none, with charity toward all, with firmness to the right as God lets us see the right, let us bind up the nations wounds.' Then he talked about a just and lasting peace. I know that I don't have his words exactly as he spoke them, but I think he had justice for all in mind."

Matt sat squirming in his seat.

"We fought those 'blue bellies' and we killed a bunch of them. I just can't see them coming down here in this reconstruction period and forgetting that we gave them the bayonet every chance we had. Even so, the final outcome was our surrender. You think they won't have vengeance in their hearts? I plan to have enough help so that we can protect as many innocent people as possible. Abraham Lincoln was shot last April, and what he said in his inaugural address means little today, but don't forget what Andrew Johnson said: 'The American people must be made to understand that treason is a crime.' Now what Lincoln said has no merit, it's what Johnson says that worries me. Tom, help me out," requested Matt.

"I remember people saying after Johnson became president that it was an act of God that a new president was sent so that Lincoln's leniency might not be put upon the people. I believe that the people of the North want to see the Southern states punished, and severely so. But President Johnson didn't change the cabinet, and Mr. Seward, who was secretary of state under Lincoln, remained secretary of state in Johnson's cabinet. He changed Johnson's mind in regard to vengeance. Both the new president and Seward agreed on a reconstruction for the south; a proclamation last May stated: "All who took part in the war against the Union must make a public statement that they will faithfully support, protect, and defend the Constitution of the United States, and keep faithfully the various laws," I replied, quoting President Johnson.

Delight was biting her upper lip, and there was a look of distress on her face.

"Oh, I was so in hopes that this bloodshed was past," she spoke in anguish. "There are some added parts to Johnson's proclamation which I feel will cause bloodshed. There were thirteen different classes of people who would not be included in the leniency clause. All governors of our states, all men educated in the Military Academy or Naval Academy who fought for the South, our prisoners of war, any person with a gross net worth of twenty thousand dollars. I don't see how it can be enforced, do you?"

"I feel that there are bad times coming to us all, for the Yankee blue belly will be given our lands and property, and will be protected by other blue belly troops. Just you mark my word," said Matt. "Tom, we need men like you here, and more so when some of these things come to pass."

"There's the Homestead Act that bothers me too," I said. "Any person of the age of twenty-one, who is an American citizen, can file on a quarter of a section of public land. But notice this: if he has borne arms against the United States, he is ineligible. That eliminates all of us in the Southern states who were in the war, yet the Northern citizen can come down here and buy the quarter section at $1.25 an acre, or eighty acres at $2.50 an acre. I believe that it's a matter of time before extra benefits are given to the Yankee soldier under that act."

Matt and I retired into the parlor to smoke while the ladies did the dishes.

"I didn't want to mention this before Delight or Bess, but I feel that soon the rangers won't have power. You know when this war broke out that, almost to the last man, we all answered Texas' call to take up arms and defend our state. We were the First Texas Ranger Regiment and, of course, were called other names as leaders came and officers fell. We became known later in the war as "Shannon's Scouts," and we especially fought Sherman as he marched across Georgia. On March 21, 1865 when all that was left of us made our last charge, we sent the enemy hightailing it. Now will we be called back to police work? Tom, I'm not sure that the rangers exist. They may right now be pardoned, but on the other hand, we may well be dispersed. I get little to no correspondence from either Austin or Houston. Both my deputy and I are aware that we may not have jobs," said Matt

"Have a sherry with me, Tom," said Matt. "I want you to ride out in the country and look this area over. You couldn't do any better than to settle right here. Our county is a fine place to live and we can pay $50 a month as marshal of the town for a good shot like you. How are you with a six-gun?"

"I'm out of practice with a six-gun. I'm only an average shot, I guess. I would like to get one of those repeaters that Sheridan's cavalry had toward the end of the war. I believe they held sixteen shots," I stated.

The women finished in the kitchen and joined us in the parlor for a few minutes. It was an excellent evening, and I said goodnight to Bess and Matt. I held Delight's hand for a minute too long—she blushed.

"I hope that we see you again," she said, as she closed the door.

In my bed at the hotel, I had trouble going to sleep. The excellent meal and the evening's conversation occupied my thoughts. I needed to make an early decision regarding the offered employment, but mostly Delight was on my mind. I just don't believe that I'd make a good lawman. A lawman was a minister of God. I went to sleep, but employment wasn't the last thing on my mind.

I BECOME A CITIZEN
OF THE AREA

I awoke thinking of Delight, for I thought she was the most beautiful, charming, and intelligent girl that I'd ever seen. Her green eyes haunted me, and I loved her dimple. I laughed when I thought of the many times she'd blushed. If there was anyone who could keep me in this area, it was Delight. I was very surprised to find that I'd slept late, and it was nearly nine thirty. I stopped at the hotel desk and asked the manager to retrieve my saddle bags from the hotel safe. There were five thousand dollars in greenbacks in the saddlebags. I breathed a sigh of relief; when the robber that stole my horse, had failed to see my saddlebags among the blankets in my sleeping area.

The bank was partially full of townspeople and business men, and I stood in line and watched Delight working. She didn't notice me until I stood second in line. She gave me a smile, and the dimple showed clearly. She was really named correctly! *What a delight she would be for some lucky guy*, I thought. I laid the saddlebags before her and took out the five thousand dollars in greenbacks. Her eyes took on a startled look as she counted the money. Greenbacks had value, but the Confederate money had lost its value completely.

"I want to open an account here," I said.

"Oh! Mr. Kirby!" she said, in a slightly alarmed voice.

Mr. Kirby, undoubtedly the manager, hurried out of his private office. He was middle-aged, and approached smiling.

"Mr. Kirby, this is Major Thomas McDowell from Virginia. He's the one who shot the robber that tried to steal his horse."

Mr. Kirby showed more interest, especially when I took from my purse a certified check in the amount of thirty-five thousand dollars.

"He wants to open an account with us," continued Delight.

"Great," said Kirby. "My, my," he said, and turning, he snapped his fingers and several employees dropped what they were doing and came to Delight's aid.

"I believe we have a total of five thousand dollars in greenbacks," said Delight.

"And what is this?" asked Mr. Kirby, looking at the check. "Major, please follow me," and he led me into his office.

The employees stood and spoke in soft tones, for there hadn't been such an amount deposited since before the war. Seated, I was served a cup of coffee, and an employee was sent to get the owner of the bank, who arrived in a short time. Mr. Robert Duncan was introduced, and he was all smiles when he learned why he'd been summoned.

"What do you want us to do with the check?" he asked.

"Deposit it into my new account with you. I may want to invest it and get it working for me," I said.

He cleared his throat. "Certainly," he stammered.

As I left the bank, I knew Delight was watching me. She was so completely distracted that she took a break and stood trembling at her window. My stomach reminded me that I hadn't had breakfast, and I hurried along the boardwalk to Sam's Restaurant. There was another restaurant at the hotel, but appeared to be not as popular. The early breakfast customers had finished their meals, and the restaurant was mostly empty. The one ranger sitting at a table nodded his head at me and, showing interest, picked up his coffee and came over to my table.

"May I join you?" he asked. "I think I know who you are! Are you the guy that shot Juan Garcia? That man's wanted for murder, robbery, gun running, you name it. I understand he was stealing your horse."

"Yes, that's his name," I answered. "I guess that was a lucky shot. It was a wonder that I didn't kill one of posse."

"I'm Ranger Wayne Crosby, and I'm new on the force," He

sipped from his coffee mug. "Our mayor wants you as town marshal, you know," he drawled.

A very pretty young waitress approached the table with a pad in her hand. "What can I get for you? We have beef steak, sausage, and eggs fixed as you like 'em. We also have some pancakes with maple syrup. Want coffee?" she inquired.

"I'll have beef steak and four eggs over lightly, and four of those pancakes and some of that maple syrup. Yes, coffee, and make it black, please."

The waitress was watching me even as she wrote my order on the pad. She had beautiful wide set blue eyes. Her hair was light brown and lay in waves down to the middle of her back. I guessed her age to be nineteen or twenty, but there was no immature behavior in her manner. Her figure was well-proportioned.

"Melody, I'll have some more coffee, if you please," said the ranger.

She dropped my order for the cook to fill and was soon back with a fresh cup for me, and a pot of steaming coffee for the ranger. She poured his coffee, and then mine. She looked up and our eyes met, but she didn't blush at all. Maybe she was used to being flirted with by all the cowboys who came in.

"Wayne, do you know this territory well? Do you know any ranches that are for sale?" I asked.

"There'll be a lot of property that must trade hands, as most of the men have been off to war and weren't able to work their places. We haven't a market for our beef, and taxes are still required. Now's the time to buy, but I'd hate to take advantage of anyone who fought for our side," he said slowly.

"I'm considering settling here, but I'm not sure what work I'll do. I've been thinking of ranching as a possibility. Are there any large ranches for sale?" I questioned.

"I'm sure you wouldn't be interested, but there's been a large Mexican ranch which is part of an old Spanish grant that may be available There are," he laughed, "only about 10,000 acres in that grant. Interested?" he asked and laughed again.

"What are they asking for it? And I was dead serious. "

His smile faded as he said, "I think they're asking $30,000. Are you still interested?" he mused.

"Do you know who could show me the place?" I questioned.

"You're kidding, aren't you?" he inquired.

"I'm as serious as I can be" I responded.

"Well, I'll be!" he said in awe, and cut off a curse word.

"I guess your going into ranching will stop you working as a marshal. Our top wages are $40 to $50 a month. Our top cowboys get about $30 a month. The town marshal's job is paying about $50 a month, but you can sleep at the jail. If you got the kind of money to buy a ranch, you don't need to be considering doing any police work," Wayne explained, with a questioning look on his face.

Melody came with my breakfast, and it didn't take long for me to dispatch the food, for I was extremely hungry. I added a second cup of coffee and paid for the meal with two bits as a tip. She smiled and her face lit for very few tipped, as money was scarce.

I followed Wayne over to the ranger's office. Matt was glad to see me, but somehow the news of my deposit had already reached his office.

"Why didn't you tell me that you were well-heeled? I feel down right ashamed that I offered you that marshal's job. Delight came by and told me on her lunch break. She goes to lunch at eleven and just left here for home," he drawled.

"Hi, Matt! I've been thinking of buying a ranch, and Wayne was telling me about the Spanish grant that's up north of town. I'm interested in seeing it. Know of anyone who might show me the boundaries?" I asked.

"Tom, you'll need a week to travel around and across that place. While I'm waiting for your wire from Austin, I could show it to you and let Wayne hold down the office here," said Matt.

Two days later, I had my two mules loaded down with supplies and extra water, as well as a new Winchester repeating rifle, and a new six-shot Colt gun on my side. Matt and I began our trip and traveled nearly a half day before Matt pointed out some rocks to be the southern end of the property. It was an excellent area for cattle. The lands were well-watered, and the grass was up to the belly of the horses. We saw several longhorn cattle and spotted wild horses throughout the region.

"All of that land bordering the north of the ranch is government land, and you are permitted to run cattle on it," said Matt, as he pointed to the north.

The ranch buildings were one story, whitewashed, adobe structures with tile roofing. There were several buildings composed of the main house, two barns, a blacksmith shop, a spring house, and a bunkhouse. Several fenced paddocks surrounded the buildings, and various horses were in them.

An older man, browned by the sun, named Don Michael Lopez received us graciously after he found the reason for our being there. The wearing of his sombrero had left a crease on his forehead, and the sun shaded half of his face. The upper skin was a shade lighter than his lower forehead and face. After Matt introduced me, Don questioned me about my major title. He shook his head as I explained my position in the Confederate army. It appeared he was angry over the outcome of the war. He explained that he wanted to move back into Mexico, as he had another ranch south of the border. The French had moved in and there was about to be trouble. Now that the Civil war was over, trouble was brewing between the French and the American army. He needed to be at his Mexican ranchero in order to retain his property.

"Señor Matt has been showing you the boundaries of my Texan ranchero. We've been watching you, and it's our opinion that you're interested in purchasing this ranch, is it not so?" asked Don.

"Si, señor," I said.

"Do you speak Spanish, amigo?" he asked.

"Un poco," I answered.

I answered, "but you speak English so well that the best Spanish that I have is poor, compared to your English."

"My price is thirty thousand dollars for the ten thousand acres. Do you have such funds? I've a map that came with my grant, made to my great grandfather by the king of Spain back in 1695, giving us this land. It has survived through various government ownerships, and is considered good today. The ranch is on the latest maps of Texas, and I believe that the deed I have, when recorded, will stand good. My horse herd will be moved to my ranch in Mexico. This area is overrun with cattle, and I cannot sell them as there isn't a market. The beef will go with the land. I hope that will be satisfactory, as I cannot move them. Ten years ago, my drovers pushed one thousand five hundred of my cattle northeast along the Shawnee Trail, and crossed the river at Red Rock, and then on to Baxter Springs. I thought it to be the thing to do, as cattle was bringing as much as forty dollars a head in Chicago. I had difficulty from the start, and lost over half my herd to Indians and to rustlers. The Texas Fever scare caused the authorities in Arkansas to quarantine the residue of my herd, and I had to pay for their upkeep during their quarantine period. I lost ninety percent of the value of my herd. Your War between the States has slowed down the market, and there was fear of different sides seizing the cattle. Most of the little ranches have lost their drovers to the war. I ain't happy with the cattle business, señor, and wish to get rid of my Texas herd."

"I don't know what I'd do with them myself, since I'm interested in horses and not cattle, but I'll pay you thirty thousand and keep the cattle, although I don't want them. To help me absorb the loss of taking the cattle, will you include one hundred head of horses with the sale?" I questioned.

"I understand your situation, amigo. I will also include one hundred head of horses with the sale," said Don.

We shook hands.

"I'll pay in northern greenbacks, and you'll hear from my lawyer as soon as arrangements can be made. As earnest money, I've a thousand dollars in greenbacks with me, and if you'll make out a bill of sale stating that you're in receipt of my thousand dollars and the balance of twenty-nine thousand to be paid at closing, we'll consider it a sale and will close as soon as the final papers are drawn up," I stated. "I'll need a couple of your men to remain here and care for my horses till I can bring some help and the transaction is closed," I requested.

"Let us go to the bunkhouse," said Don. "I have two Texans who might be of help."

The bunkhouse was a cool, well-built adobe whitewashed

building. Three or four sleeping cowboys were in their bunks and they didn't stir when Don and I entered, followed by Matt.

"Where are Paul and Rex, por favor?" asked Don.

"Here I am," cried Paul. "Rex rode herd last night and is asleep yet."

Paul shook Rex awake. When told of the real estate transaction, both men wanted to stay on under the new ownership, and the arrangements were made. Paul appeared to be the older of the two, and was told to oversee the horses until the estate closure.

"Paul has much experience in buying and selling horses. I often send him on my buying trips and he knows what I need and does the buying for me," explained Don. "Paul can help select the hundred horses, if you don't mind. You'll select a horse; then Paul will select a horse for me, and so on, until the one hundred head is decided. Isn't that a fair way to make the decision?" he asked.

"I'll watch the selections and have the final decision on any horse that Paul selects for me," I suggested.

"Si, it appears all right with me, señor," answered Don. "I've a dozen or so prime horses set aside for my herd in Mexico, which I want to retain. They will not be included in the sale, señor."

"Agreed!" I said.

I took a hundred dollars in greenbacks and left it with Paul, telling him to buy what they'd need. I'd keep in touch with them. I added that I may be back prior to settlement; there were a few things I saw that needed to be looked after, and soon.

Matt didn't say a word until we left the hacienda and started back toward his home and my hotel. Finally, after a few miles in silence, Matt spoke up.

"Believe you got the best of that deal, Tom. I've no idea just what you'll do with those cattle. They keep the rivers muddy and you can find at least four thousand head in the rivers right now clear up to their hips. I know that there are at least a thousand head of wild horses around too. My question is, will the Don consider them as his and try to drive them south? Now that hundred head of horses will make you some money, but it'll be awhile before it'll pay off," drawled Matt. "Here, I was thinking you would be my ranger, not expecting that you'd be a rancher."

The journey home was uneventful and it was good to be back in town. It was Saturday, and Delight had finished work for the day. I followed Matt to his house, and asked if I could see Delight. She came to the door and invited me into the parlor.

"I owe you a dinner," I said. "May I take you to dinner at the restaurant? Do you like the restaurant better than the hotel?"

"Let's go to the restaurant tonight," she said. "I'm hungry!"

"I'll pick you up at seven," I said. "It'll give me a chance to shower and shave and change clothing."

I stopped at the livery stable and rented a steel-wheeled surrey. "Have it ready for me at 6:45," I said.

I rushed to the hotel for a bath, shave, and clean clothes. I polished my boots and was at the livery at 6:45 for the surrey and rented horse. Delight had planned on walking to the restaurant, and was pleasantly surprised to see me at the door, and the surrey with horse tied at the hitching rail.

"Now, isn't that something?"

She smiled, and her dimple made her a delight in my eye. I helped her up into the buggy, and we soon were at the restaurant. There were three or four buggies tied to the hitching rack, as well as half a dozen horses. Melody stared at us as we came in. I nodded to her, and she blushed. It was the first time that I'd seen her blush. Delight had seen our exchange of glances.

"Oh, do you know Melody?" she inquired. "We're old friends and have been since we were children in school together."

We found a comfortable table near a window, and Melody came with her pad. She looked tired; she'd been working all day. Saturday was a special time for the residents of the town to have an evening out. As I sat there, I began to compare the two girls, Delight appeared to have a slight advantage. We ate a good meal, and then I asked Delight if she would like to ride some. She agreed, and we moved though the town at a slow trot. As we went by the jail, Matt and Wayne waved to us. Matt appeared to be unconcerned, but I saw him watching us till we were lost from his sight.

"May I drive?" she asked.

"Sure, but be careful, as this is a new horse to me and I've no idea just how skittish he might be," I said, as I turned over the reins to Delight.

She drove west on the road until we were out of sight from the lamp light of the houses. The sky was vast and every star appeared to be visible. Texas was prodigious, beautiful, historic, and now my home.

"Whoa!" she said, and the horse came to a stop.

She tied the reins to the front board of the surrey.

"Tom, Dad told me that you bought the Spanish ranch today. I know that you're not interested in staying here now. Dad and I wanted so much for you to settle down here, and everyone was rooting for you to make up your mind to remain here. I'm so disappointed."

"Delight, I've never met a girl like you. The war put me out of reach of women. Because of the war, I lost a girl named Audrey back home. I really planned to call on her following the war, but she married while I was away. That was my only girlfriend, although I did some dancing at balls when I was a captain and the war permitted such events. When you came in from work the other night, I was really smitten and have been ever since. I believe that I love you," I confessed. She turned toward me, and I could see her face. Her green eyes were focused on me. Her countenance was stern and serious. These were tender moments and something very meaningful had been said to her. As I sat there waiting, her face beamed with joy and acceptance.

"Oh, Tom, are you sure? We haven't given this enough time! I saw you looking at Melody, who is such a pretty girl. Are you sure? Could it be possible that in these few days since we've met, you could possibly be in love with me?"

"Delight, I knew when I first saw you and stood staring like an idiot at you in your home that you were the one for me."

"Oh, Tom," and she came into my arms.

Our embrace was tender, and the kiss that followed was ecstasy to both of us. She gave as much tenderness as she received.

"Your dad sure named you right!" I said. "Delight, I've bought a huge ranch, and plan to work it the rest of my life. Would you share my life with me? Would you be my wife?"

"Yes," was her simple answer.

I kissed her again and again.

"Enough, please, Tom! We must get back, for Dad will be looking for us."

She picked up the reins and clucked at the horse and turned it around toward town.

Tom thought of what she had said as they rode toward town. Soldiers deprived of female companionship often seek permanent security in marriage. Many a soldier becomes engaged during a furlough, or upon the war's end quick to ask for the hand of his girl-friend in marriage. Doubts have a tendency to follow a proposal, and engagement time often ends without marriage. *Should I have given this more time as she suggested?* I wondered.

BETROTHED! BUT I'M NOT SO SURE!

News of our betrothal swept the town. I found out later that it wasn't expected at all. Delight had been dating a soldier, Captain Fred Dyer, in the Hood brigade of Longstreet's division. They had grown up together, and it was common knowledge that she'd indicated to him that she'd wait. When I heard this, I was really concerned if I'd done the right thing. Her friend was a captain and had been captured. No one knew why he'd not returned when the war was over. Most of the defeated army had found their way back home by now. I began to relive those moments when I was in the bank, depositing my check and greenbacks. I still could remember the look that was in her eyes. *Was that greed I saw? No, I don't think so. I believe it was surprise. Yes, that's it! She was amazed, and couldn't believe what she was seeing.* Our old preacher used to quote the words of Paul as he wrote to Timothy: "For the love of money is the root of all evil: while some coveted after, they have erred from the faith, and pierced themselves through with many sorrows."

When she asked to drive the surrey, did she have in her mind getting me alone and encouraging me by driving to that isolated area? I was beginning to doubt if I'd done the right thing. The next morning, I went into the restaurant for an early breakfast. Melody at first appeared aloof, but then she approached me with her pad and pencil.

"What'll you have today? We've the usual, except the cook has put fried potatoes and grits on the menu."

She didn't appear to be upset.

"Give me bacon and four eggs, fried potatoes, and grits, with plenty of coffee, and black as usual. I want four of those hot cakes too, with your good maple syrup," I said.

"What's this I've heard about you popping the question last night?" she asked in a sly way and looked at me over the pad. "Delight is a fine girl," she added.

"Yes, Melody, I bought a ranch up north, and I sure need a good wife. Plan to fill that hacienda with little ones."

"Do you know about Fred Dyer?" she asked. "Did Delight say anything about him? They grew up together, and it has been the consensus that they'd planned to marry when he gets home."

"No, Melody, Delight didn't mention him. But I've been told, three times now, about their love for each other. I wish he was back from the war so I could meet him," I said.

Melody seemed chastised by my remarks, and quickly took her pad to the kitchen.

After breakfast, I let it be known that I was interested in at least a dozen cowboys to work for me at my ranch.

I stopped by the bank and asked if the certified check had cleared. It should be clear in two weeks, was the answer. I hired a lawyer to try to check the title that Don would have ready at closing. Everything appeared to be progressing nicely. Soon I had no less than twenty good cowboys who were interested in working for me.

Delight was interested in marrying right away, but I told her that the house needed a lot of repair and beautifying. It needed a woman's touch, but I didn't tell her that. Delight appeared to be upset. She told her mother and dad that she'd keep her job until the marriage. Bess made plans to have the marriage at the hacienda when the house was complete, and agreed with me that we should have the house in good shape so Delight could be married in her home. There were twelve rooms in the hacienda, and they'd support many overnight guests.

FRED DYER COMES HOME

George Cavenaugh rode up to the front of the hacienda, and tied his horse at the gate. George had been delayed from joining us when we left Big Spring due to some tutoring he needed to finish. I had agreed to his delay of a week when I hired him. I invited George into my study where he made the following report:

"Fred Dyer came home. He'd been wounded in the last month of the war, and convalescence had been rather lengthy. Now, six weeks later, I saw him ride his horse into town and tie it to a hitching post in front of the bank. He still wore his butternut uniform, and smelt of the prison and of the trail. I happened to be in the bank to get some cash from my tutoring work. What I tell you is mostly from my observation, as well as Matt's message to you.

"He limped into the bank, and several customers recognized him. He approached Delight, came around behind her teller window, and, catching her hand, pulled her to him. She wasn't expecting him, and he kissed her on the lips. She pushed him away, and her eyes blazed with anger. She saw who it was, and let him kiss her again. Other workers at the bank gathered around and welcomed him back home. Delight stood there, completely disturbed and unsure what to do. It was very apparent that he didn't know of Delight's engagement to you. Mr. Kirby came from his office and took Delight aside. I could hear his remarks, and most standing in line at the Teller's window could too," said George.

"'Delight, I think you two have some talking to do,' he said.

'May I have the rest of the day off, Mr. Kirby?'

'I think you owe it to Fred to tell him as soon as possible, don't you? Yes, go on home.'

"This ends what I saw and heard. The balance of this report comes from Matt," stated George. "Here is his note to you." George handed me a note written in pencil I opened it and read:

Tom, Fred Dyer came home. I saw him and Delight approaching the house so I rode ahead of them. Delight told him about you, and it greatly angered him. He made threats on your life so I followed him to the Last Chance Saloon, where further threats were made with his friends about you. They said they would help him cause bodily harm to you. Watch out!

"Thanks, George for your concern. I'll keep this note and thank Matt later for the warning." I said. "Welcome to the TM ranch. I'll call Paul, my foreman, and he'll get you settled in."

•

When I arrived back at the hacienda, I found my two hired hands busy caring for the horses. They were breaking them to saddle and bridle, as well as to saddle blankets. Some of the horses were already broken, and they'd been separated and put in other paddocks. Most of the horses were above average stock, and were good, gentle animals. I began to clean the hacienda and the bunkhouse, and I put a fresh coat of whitewash on all the buildings. The adobe structures needed refreshing. I checked carefully the red tile roofs of all the structures. Fences were mended and everything increased in beauty and utility. I got my grumbling crew out into the hay fields, where they cut with scythes the standing hay. They loaded the hay on wagons and lifted them, with hay forks and rope and tackle, into the barns. It took them nearly a month to get all the hay into the barns. The ranch was well-prepared in case there was a harsh winter.

The cowboys rode into the fields and came in to report the sighting of hundreds of wild horses, as well as cows and bulls. I began to build more holding pens, in the event that I might be able to round up some of the wild horses.

•

One morning, in early September, I awoke early and rode out on my blue mare to scout the territory to the west. In the distance, I could make out the blue outlines of a mountain range. I knew that my range didn't extend that far west, but I was interested in that section of land. I'd ridden about five miles, when I came across the shod prints of four horses. I could see that they weren't Indians, and they were headed in the same direction that I was. As I came near to a creek, I smelled smoke, and was careful as I approached a camp.

"Hello, the camp! May I come in?"

Four men were breaking camp and were in the process of throwing water on their fire.

"Fellows, please be sure to get that fire out, for I've a lot of grass, and it runs all the way to my house and outbuildings."

"Fred, it's him! We've got him now. He's cornered!" cried one of the four.

Fred reached out and caught my arm and pulled me from my grulla. The other three jumped me, and by their weight held me down.

"What's this all about?" I asked.

"Mister," said Fred, "I'm going to beat you to death. You stole my girl, and I've nothing left in my life."

"You must be Fred Dryer," I said. "I didn't know you existed until after she said yes to me. I love her, and if I thought she'd have me, I'd have asked her knowing you were a suitor."

Fred swung a hard right at my face as I lay there, pinned by the other three. I managed to move my head enough for his fist to just brush my cheek. He let out an oath, for his fist had struck a large rock in the soil. I was now kicking and swinging on my own. My upper body strength and broad chest were overpowering to my attackers. I gained my feet, and fought as I'd been trained in the service. I kicked one and poked the eyes of another. They had me by both my arms, and Fred was trying with his good fist to deal punishment to me.

I heard the swish of an arrow, and the arrow went almost completely through the body of one of the men holding me. There was another thud as another arrow went through the throat of a second fighter. My two remaining attackers jumped behind trees with drawn pistols. There were darting Apaches coming on us from all sides. Fred's friends knew how to fight, for they'd just come home from four years of warfare. One threw me my pistol, and we began to fire at any Apache that we saw. Fred was shot point blank by an Apache with a rifle. He fell into the smoldering fire, but didn't feel it. He was dead before he hit the flame. The remaining friend of Fred's and I got to our horses, and I drew my new Winchester rifle and poured lead into the approaching Apaches. I shot six times, and there were five dead Indians lying in front of us. I'd shot one twice due to my rapid fire. With a scream of anger, the Apaches turned and fled.

"I'm Warren Lee," said the remaining white man. "You saved us both with rapid fire from that Winchester. I've never seen a man that could fire that fast and not miss a shot. I know now why you've the respect of the posse, for I've never seen such shooting."

"Let's tie your friends onto their horses and get them back to the ranch, Warren, I was hoping that we could find peace with the Apache. Now it appears that they're on the war path."

We rode hard and fast, in case the Apaches were following. It was dark when we got back to the ranch. I woke three cowboys, and put them on guard duty while I explained what'd happened to my full crew of cowboys.

"Warren, you can bed down here tonight, and we'll see what tomorrow brings. I want you to make a full report to the rangers when you get back to town. I'll send help with you so you can get your friends back to Big Spring and to their families," I said. "I want Paul and Rex to help out here with carrying these bodies back to town. Paul, I also want you to take a note in to Delight to explain about Fred's death and how he was killed. Warren, be sure that you tell the ranger how it happened," I said. "I don't want anyone in town to believe that I killed Fred. I'm very sorry about this misunderstanding."

The next morning, the three carried the bodies back to town. Delight got my letter and wept over Fred. Matt got the news and put some of the blame on himself for failing to stop Fred from his attempt.

"For Tom's sake, if Fred had to die, I'm glad the Apaches did the killing and not Tom," said Matt.

Delight wanted to know if the house was about ready. Rex said that everything was looking very good, but I'd said I wouldn't want our guests out there with the Apaches on the warpath, so the wedding was put off, and winter set in. I sent word that the wedding would now have to be put off until spring. Delight was very unhappy for the delay, and began to wonder if I was having cold feet with all the excuses. Her dad told her that he understood my concern.

THE ARMY INVESTIGATES
FRED'S DEATH

It was two weeks later, that Paul knocked at the door of the hacienda.

"Tom. There's a troop of Yankee cavalry coming up the road."

"I wonder what they want. Have the boys stay out of sight, and don't let anyone show anger while the Yankees are here. Understand?"

When the detail rode up to the house, the lieutenant introduced himself.

"Good morning, sir, I am First Lieutenant Joseph L. Grady; I presume that I am speaking to Thomas McDowell?"

"That's right. I'm Tom McDowell, and what can I do for you?"

"We received a report that three men were killed by Apaches in this area. The report came from . . ." he looked down at a paper, "Ranger Matt Willard. I understand that you were one of those who fought the savages and inflicted some severe punishment."

"Lieutenant, we fought for our lives and managed to get away, but they killed three of our party. There was no reason to warrant such an attack on their part, and we were fortunate to make an escape."

"I've been instructed to see if I can find the warring party, arrest them, and take them in for possible punishment."

"Lieutenant, there's no way that you can track them. The event occurred about a month ago. I can show you on the map of my place approximately where it happened. I'm not sure that I can find the exact place myself," I stated. "I hope that you know this area, for it appears that snow is expected soon. They tell me that these Northerners can bring on some bad blizzards."

"May I see your map? Sergeant, come with me; I want you to see this too," stated the officer.

A large first sergeant, in an overcoat, followed the officer into my study. With a pencil, I tried to mark the approximate place where the attack took place on the map of my property.

"There are some trees along here, near the river, and we were near the edge when they attacked us."

"Would it be possible for you to go with us?" asked the lieutenant.

"If I could be of service, I'd be glad to go," I said. "But as I said, I don't believe I can find the place. It was my first trip into that area. There are three houses that belong to me that have been used in the past as line shacks. I was up there looking for them, and they're not where I thought them to be."

"We'll get along fine, as I've a couple scouts who know this area. I believe we can find where the attack took place," said the lieutenant, but his disappointment was evident.

"If your detail runs into a blizzard, you'll have a place of refuge right here."

•

Later, the big first sergeant told me the details of the trip to find the battle area where Fred and his friends were killed:

"The troop was only about one hour out when the Northerner struck. The storm started with a driving, cold rain, and quickly turned to sleet. Our squad was in their ponchos and leaned into the wind and sleet. The wind was howling and a fine snow interlaced with the sleet. I said to the lieutenant:

'Sir, this has all the earmarks of being one bad storm. Do you think we should turn back and take Mr. McDowell at his word?'

The lieutenant agreed, and our troop turned south."

•

I wasn't surprised to see the troop return to the ranch. I put on my poncho and went to the bunkhouse, where I prepared my men for our guests.

"Fellows, we're going to have company. These are Yankees, and we'll treat them as company until this blizzard is finished. It's a really bad storm, and giving them shelter may save them from death."

"Six months ago, I wouldn't mind knocking off a few, and even using my bayonet," drawled one of the Texans.

"I believe that we can handle twenty in here, and we'll take the officers and non-commissioned on to the main house. I expect you all to be on good behavior."

Coming out of the bunkhouse, I heard the same type of advice spoken by the lieutenant to his squad of twenty-five troops. I told him my plans on how to divide the troop. The horses were crowded into the two barns, and the troopers dried them by rubbing them down. In the bunkhouse, troopers and cowboys gathered near the pot-bellied stove, and introduced themselves to one another. Paul assigned each trooper a bunk, and they appeared very happy and content to be out of the storm. Paul saw to it that the troop cook had a place in the main house to help with the cooking. I showed the officers and non-commissioned officers where they'd sleep. Rooms were opened that'd been prepared for the wedding guests. The chuck wagon was parked at the kitchen door, and large coffee pots were soon filled with black, steaming coffee. The two cooks sat down together to plan the meals of the coming days.

The storm howled for three days, and the snow drifted around the buildings up to three feet deep. The cowboys had to get out into the snow and carry hay to the horses in the paddocks. Some cattle were bawling from hunger in the fields, and I sent the cowboys with additional hay.

"I just can't let anything go hungry if I can help it. I nearly starved in the trenches at Petersburg," I said.

When the storm was over, it had lasted three days, the weather cleared up quickly; the sun was out, and it was warm in a few hours. The troopers were very thankful for the refuge, and the cowboys found they'd made friends they'd have for some time. It was during these days of confinement that the first sergeant told me how the troop had run into the storm and had to turn back. The troop really appreciated getting in out of the blizzard.

"Six months ago, I'd have shot them, but now I'm glad I didn't," drawled Rex.

"Check on our livestock, men!" I requested. "Save as many as you can." I had fears that calves and some of the younger stock might be trapped in the deep snow.

"You know, Tom, you've some really good horses here. Want to sell any of them? I see you haven't branded any, but do you have a bill of sale for them?" asked the lieutenant. "I'll see the major when I get back to the fort and send one of my men back in case he's interested and can make a deal."

I grinned. "Got them in the deal when I bought this place, and I do have a bill of sale! Yes, I'll sell you what you need if we can agree on a price."

The troop turned west again, knowing that the storm had completely erased any old signs of where the three white men had been killed. I now knew where I could market my horses, and just maybe, I might be able to sell a few head of cattle. For the next two weeks, the cowboys were busy feeding hay to cattle and horses alike. The troop returned to their fort in New Mexico. A couple weeks later, a dispatch came with an offer to buy one hundred horses, and I was well pleased with the offer. My cowboys made plans to drive the horses to the fort when weather permitted. A later request came asking for a thousand head of cattle, and it was an exceptional offer. The United States Army appeared to be happy in the way my cowboys and I had shown friendship to the lieutenant and his troopers. Plans were formulated for horses and cattle to be delivered and the cattle to be branded. I would make an application for a brand, and Paul would have the irons made and brought back from town. Branding could commence as soon as Paul got back. Of course, I could see Delight, and I found myself very apprehensive for some reason. The ranch was far from other towns and the nearest one was Big Spring; I could have no way of communication with Delight, as there was no mail. I prepared for my trip to Big Spring.

I'd stay at the hotel and visit with Matt and Bess and see Delight. I thought of eating at the restaurant and seeing Melody too. Why'd I think of Melody? It was her face that I saw, especially the way she took my order and looked over the pad at me. Sweet, good-natured Melody was in my thoughts. Maybe that was why I'd made so many excuses to postpone the wedding. If only I didn't feel I was trapped into asking Delight to marry me.

Paul and I rode into Main Street and tied our horses in front of the hotel. Matt had seen us as we passed by the jail, and hurried down to catch us before we could enter the hotel.

"Hello, Tom! Hi, Paul," greeted the ranger. "What brings you two into town?"

I tied my horse to the hitching post and turned toward the ranger.

"Hello, Matt! Glad to see you. How are Bess and Delight?"

"We're all fine, but don't want another one of those Northerners this year. It's good that we held up the wedding until spring. Can you imagine what it would've been like to have all those guests stranded between here and the ranch," commented Matt.

"Don't even mention it," I pleaded. "Matt, where do I make an application for a brand? I want Paul to get to work having them made so he can start back to the ranch in the morning."

"Come on, Tom, and I'll show you," said Matt.

I started after Matt; then turned toward Paul.

"Paul, sign us in at the hotel, and carry our saddle bags up to the room. It shouldn't take long to make this application," I stated.

Matt led me to the proper office, where the application was completed and a TM design was indicated for the brand. Paul looked at the design, which hooked together the two letters for Tom McDowell.

"Got it," he said, and was off toward the blacksmith shop to have several sets of irons made. I told Matt about the troop getting trapped by the storm, and how well things had worked out with the selling of the horses and cattle, and the need for the branding irons.

"Tom, that was pure luck; several ranches in this area have cattle and no outlet," indicated Matt.

"Luck? No, Matt, not luck; I depend in faith on my Lord!"

Matt looked toward his shoes for a few moments. He didn't know what to say.

"Tom, I looked to him in prayer a few times during the war or I don't think I would've made it."

"Matt, I came through that Pickett charge with a shattered rifle, a hole in my canteen, and six bullet holes through my trousers and remember praying continuously. You know Paul told the Thessalonians to 'Pray without ceasing,' and I did!" I grinned. "I still pray about the first Yank that I shot. He was just a kid in a man's body, but I watched the light go out in his eyes. I have dreams of that horrible moment and see his lifeless face. He has always that look of amazement on his face, and there're other blue coats behind him that I shot but didn't see their faces. May the Lord help me to erase those moments from my memory. I had to shoot or they'd have killed me or one of my troop. War is terrible, isn't it?"

Matt stood there still looking downward and finally said, "Tom, we've all bad memories that came out of that war."

THE TM RANCH

"I'm happy for your good fortune, but I've some bad news, Tom," Matt said, as I walked up to his front porch. "Austin has refused payment of the thousand dollar reward money. They claim that there's inadequate funds, and have even asked me to halt trying to hire any new rangers. I'm not sure, but I might have to let Wayne go. There's talk that the entire ranger organization may be banned. I could be without a job myself. Bess isn't at home right now; she is at the church at a missionary meeting. She'll be upset that she couldn't prepare dinner for you tonight."

"It's my turn to be the host. Before she gets started on your evening meal, tell her that I want you two, along with Paul and Delight, to eat with me at the restaurant. Boy, I've got to wash away a ton of dirt, and I've not shaved today. See you at 6:00? Isn't that the time you usually eat?" I asked.

He nodded his agreement. "That'll be fine, Tom."

I walked into the hotel and expressed my greetings to the manager and his clerk. I got the keys to my room, and asked for fresh water for a bath. I shaved and slipped by the barber shop to get a haircut. I walked toward the blacksmith shop, where I saw for the first time just what my brand would look like.

"Paul," I said. "I understand that out here, a cowboy works for the brand. We are now the TM outfit."

"Congratulations, boss," said Paul. "I think we'll be known all through this area as the TM Ranch."

"Paul, I've asked Matt, Bess, and Delight to eat with us at the restaurant. Get you a bath, and shave that beard. You're just a bit raunchy, you know," I said, grinning. "Here's a ten in case you're short on cash."

"Well, I'll get to see Melody!" Paul said.

It was like a punch landing just below the belt. I hadn't even thought that he might be interested in Melody. Paul rushed up to our room and soon was singing as he scrubbed his feet and splashed water from the tub. He'd paid the extra twenty-five cents for the fresh water too, so he didn't use my bath water. He laid out his best shirt, which was the only other shirt he owned, and shaved his face clean. It was the first time I'd seen his face without a partial beard. *A really fine-looking young man,* I thought. *Melody will look twice at him.* Jealousy was a green-eyed monster, but I'd no right to envy him. *Say,* I thought, *maybe I can get him interested in Delight. He hasn't enough money for Delight to be interested in him.* My heart sank as I wondered why I thought like that. *Wasn't it true?*

I'd sent a rented surrey down to pick up Matt, Bess, and Delight. Paul and I walked over and we arrived just as the surrey pulled up to the hitching post. I paid the surrey driver and told him I'd be responsible for the rig. My breath was taken away as Delight rushed from the surrey into my arms. What a beautiful girl, and she was my betrothed. Her green eyes were bright and she kissed me right there in front of the restaurant.

"Delight!" cried Bess in alarm.

"Who cares, Mom?" spoke out Delight. "Everyone knows we're to be married come spring."

She really knew how to kiss. Her smile flashed her dimple, and suddenly I was wondering if I'd misjudged her. I hugged her to me and then we were joined by her dad and mother, and together we went into the restaurant. Seated by her side with Matt and Bess on my left, I looked past her to Paul. His face was red as he saw the menu and the prices.

"Today, Delight, I named our ranch the TM Ranch. TM stands for Tom McDowell," I said. She looked alarmed, and very upset, and I saw that an explanation was needed. "TM is our brand, so we can show ownership on our cattle and horses," I explained.

She knew what I meant, and still there was hurt and anger in her eyes.

Bess, Matt, and Paul saw the change in her face, and Matt went on to explain that I had to acquire the brand in order to sell my horses and cattle.

"Why didn't you name the ranch the TM/DW ranch? That way my name would be on there too?" she asked.

Matt frowned and Bess put her hand to her mouth. Paul was amazed and looked from her to me. I was uneasy, but I showed my anger.

"Delight, I'll run the business end of the ranch. You'll run the house!" I said with finality.

Matt smiled, and Bess looked pleased, and Paul hid a grin behind his hand. Delight looked as if she'd been shot.

"Hear me, Tom McDowell! I work every day with figures and business at the bank, and I'm looked up to for what I do. Please don't speak disparagingly of me. Don't leave me out of decisions," she added rather softly.

"I'm sorry if I offended you. Please forgive me. What I've done, I've done, and the name will remain as it is. I'll share with you when we're married. Your name will be there with mine. We'll share good times and some difficult ones, and I'll take you as you must take me, for better or for worse. As the church and our Lord is one, so shall you and I be one. Do you agree?" I asked.

Her eyes were big and luminous. They softened and she smiled.

"Yes," she whispered.

Melody was at my side, and asked us, "Are you ready to order?"

I looked up to see Matt nodding yes and Bess brushing a tear from her eyes.

"Indeed, we are," said Paul, and he smiled into Melody's face.

"We've meat loaf as a special tonight, and it's our cook's extra good recipe," Melody said. "Its fifty cents, but that includes your drink and dessert."

"Sounds good to me," said Bess, and we all agreed we'd have the same.

"Food prices are increasing. I remember when we could get a good meal for thirty cents," said Matt.

What Matt had told me about the rangers and his financial problems, brought to my mind Delight's possible lack of money.

"Are you all right? Do you need money as you prepare for the wedding?"

I was embarrassed, for it appeared as if she didn't have money for her marriage preparation.

"I'm fine and have saved a long time to be ready for marriage," she said. "Tom, let's set the date now. Shall we set it for May 10th? That'll be a Saturday, and our guests can drive out in the morning, and we can have dinner for them and can have our marriage at two o'clock. If some need to get home, they'll have a good five hours to ride back, and we can have our reception for those who can stay. Oh Tom, let me plan with you, for this is so special to me," she declared.

My heart melted as I looked at her. I slipped her hand into mine under the table and I squeezed lightly. *My, my, what a woman,* I thought.

Then I quietly said, "May the 10th will be fine, honey!"

"Paul, do you want another piece of pie?" asked Melody.

"Yes, please," he drawled, "and more coffee."

I took the bill and followed Melody to the desk. I tipped her well and watched her as she looked at the added money and smiled her thanks.

"Thank you, sir, err, Tom," she said. Her smile lighted her face.

"You all ready to head home?" I asked of Matt and Bess.

I took up the reins after I'd helped Delight into the surrey and took Matt and Bess home. Delight didn't move and I knew that she wanted to talk more. Paul had stayed at the restaurant and was drinking more coffee and laughing with Melody.

"You kids want to come into the parlor?" asked Matt. "It's terribly cold."

"I believe that would be best," I said.

Delight sat with me on the divan and said, "Tom, I'm sorry about our misunderstanding at supper. I love you so, but things haven't been moving as I wanted them. I desired so much to get married this fall, and here it's December. May is five months away, and it seems so long. Hold me, honey."

And I did. Delight was a very beautiful girl. Her kisses were promises, and held spirit.

"Paul and I must get back to the ranch early, for we've those irons and we need to be branding both horses and cattle," I said.

Matt, Bess, and Delight all said they appreciated the very special evening. Melody had a room off the kitchen at the back of restaurant.

A MOST DELIGHTFUL CHRISTMAS

"Will you be here for Christmas?" Delight asked as I started to leave.

"I've hopes that your Dad would get this surrey and bring you and your mother out. If you'll agree, I'll make arrangements for the surrey for three days, say the 24th, 25th, and 26th," I stated.

We stepped into the kitchen and invited Matt and Bess to the ranch for Christmas. They were looking forward to seeing the house, and appreciated the invitation.

"Tom, I want you to be on the lookout for Juan Garcia. He's the man you shot; I got a flyer that states he broke jail and has two with him. The last we heard, they were in Arizona. Juan's left arm is stiff from your shot, and he swears he'll kill you before he's caught. Tom, he and those with him are the kind that would shoot you in the back if they got a chance. He's part Apache and may seek shelter among Apache people. Your north river borders land used by the Apache, so again I say, be careful," Matt said.

Later, I told Paul about Juan being on the loose, and to remind me to alert the cowboys.

"Our men need to carry their rifles when they're on the range. Paul, do they all have rifles? Maybe we need to buy some more of those repeaters like I used on the Apache. The 1866 Winchester is better than the Henry used by the Union cavalry during the war," I said.

•

The next morning, we were at the restaurant early and had our bacon, eggs, fried potatoes, and flapjacks. The maple syrup added excellent flavor. Melody was a very pleasing and smiling young lady, and paid more attention to Paul than she had the night before. He'd made headway after we'd left him at the restaurant, when he'd had her to himself. I paid for the breakfast and gave her a dollar tip, which brought her a smile.

"Thanks," she whispered to me. She raised her voice to Paul. "Merry Christmas. If I don't see you before then, you and boss man have a very merry Christmas."

Paul and I in chorus said, "Merry Christmas!"

We left the restaurant ready for the day, and rode warily along the trail toward the ranch. The trail was a part of the Comanche War Trail, which ran to and forked at Big Spring. The town received its name from its location, and the history of the trail told of battles fought there by various Indian tribes. The U.S. army was known to stop there, and Texas Rangers lived in the vicinity. In 1839, Dr. Henry Connelly, a trader from Mexico with a fortune in silver, passed through this location on his way to Oklahoma.

We arrived at the ranch right at noon, and the cowboys were waiting for the branding irons. Rex took one of the irons and stuck it into the pot bellied stove, and pressed the red hot iron into the threshold of the bunkhouse door. The TM was ablaze for a minute, and the crew stood watching. A brown and black TM was left on the door.

"Fellows," said Rex. "We're the TM Ranch, and we work for the brand." He raised his coffee cup and cried, "Long live the TM Ranch. We're the toughest, meanest bunch of cowboys this side of the Pecos."

I stood there and grinned at them.

"We're one for all, and all for one. We're family. Isn't any Indian, rustler, or Yankee blue belly going to run over us, right? Right! Listen to me now and hear me out! Juan Garcia has broken out of jail and may be in this area. There are two riding with him that may be half breeds, or may be full blooded Apache. He's the guy that I shot off my horse. He may be living among the Apache tribes north of us. If you ride out on our range, go in pairs, or by threes, and take a Winchester with you. Don't take any chances. I bought four new Winchesters today, and fifty boxes of shells. I want each of you to demonstrate how you can shoot. If you've any bad shooting habits, I want them corrected, for your life and mine depend upon how accurate we are. When you can consistently hit a bull's eye dead center at a hundred yards, I'll raise your pay to sixty dollars a month and give you one of those new Winchesters. My whole squad in Company A were sharpshooters," I told them.

The TM crew was determined to get a raise and a new Winchester, and competition was keen. Paul and Rex were the first to earn Winchesters, and before Christmas, they'd all earned their awards. I had their names engraved on their Winchester and left them in the boxes in which they'd arrived. Christmas was going to be a special day at the TM Ranch. I'd present them their guns and bonuses then. Each cowboy was given a room to clean, for they hadn't been cleaned since the Yankees had stayed in them for three days during the storm. All grumbled, fussed, and fumed, but they cleaned and scrubbed until floors, walls, and furniture were clean and polished. I must say that they did a good job and worked until they were satisfied with the finished job. They acted like it was a calamity for a cowboy to do such work, but were ashamed if the clean room didn't meet the standard set by Rex or Paul.

The cook cleaned the kitchen till all the pots and pans were reflecting the light of the sun. The silverware was cleaned and placed neatly back into its cartons. I had one of the cowboys go into the pasture and bring back a Christmas tree. I worked at decorating it myself with popcorn that I strung on thread and used some cotton to imitate snow on the branches.

Matt, Bess, and Delight arrived on Christmas Eve, right at noon, in the surrey. Bess and Delight were intrigued by the hacienda, and Matt went into the barns and stood in the cold wind to stare at the horses in the paddock. He was especially interested in an Appaloosa, which stood fifteen hands high. The horse had intelligent eyes and had good breeding. Matt looked at the animal's teeth and found him to be young and gentle, yet powerful in stature.

There was hot apple cider, and I'd warned my crew they weren't to drink alcoholic beverages or use profane language around the house. The cook baked six hens with stuffing and prepared potatoes, corn, cabbage, and apples. He baked ten pies and four cakes, one of which was a flop, but still he iced it. It looked good, even though it had a few bulges, which he'd tried to smooth over. The cowboys had been practicing singing *Silent Night*. There was one cowboy who had a harmonica and played *Jingle Bells*. All the men were invited to the hacienda, and they came shaved and clean, wearing their good shirts. Each of the men got his new rifle and an envelope with seventy dollars in it. The extra ten was a bonus for working so hard. Bess was surprised to receive a gold comb, and Matt had a note with a bill of sale for the Appaloosa he'd admired so much.

I teased Delight by saying, "Oh, darling, I forgot and left your gift at the hotel."

She knew better and smiled while I brought out her diamond engagement ring. The cowboys all moaned and groaned as she embraced and kissed me. I got a new shirt from Matt and Bess, Delight gave me a sweater, and the cowboys pooled their money to purchase me a new Colt forty-four revolver and holster. Slim Wilkins, who was the best of the group with a six-gun, promised me that he'd teach me the fast draw. All the cowboys chided me at being so slow. We all joined in to sing Christmas carols as the cook looked over his new cookbook. The cook led us into the dining room, where dinner was served. I surprised them all by offering thanks for Jesus Christ and the love of God that he gave at Christmas. Things got very still and then all said "amen." TM Ranch had become a home for twenty cowboys, a cook, a couple who would soon marry, a ranger, and a very sweet mother-in-law.

Matt saddled the Appaloosa with the new saddle, saddle blanket, and bridle. He rode ahead of the surrey as Bess and Delight took turns driving on their way back to town. Bess and Delight sang and laughed while they reminisced of the actions of various cowboys. It was the best Christmas they'd ever had.

"Mother, did you hear Tom pray? Was I ever surprised!" Delight said.

"Honey, I believe you've a very special person there. He'll make a good husband, and I believe that he loves you very much," Bess said, as she turned her attention to her driving.

Delight sat and quietly wept, and when Bess noticed her, she put her arms around her daughter.

"Happy, Delight?" she asked.

"Oh, Mother, I didn't know what true love was until just recently. I feel like my heart is so full that surely it'll burst."

Matt had turned and watched them over his shoulder; what he saw were tears of happiness. He looked down at the Appaloosa and gave him a pat, for he sure liked his horse. Matt made note to tell me of the trip and its consequences. The next time he saw me he relished the telling of the return trip home.

Back at the ranch, I sat in a chair and saw in my mind's eye my betrothed as she looked with shining eyes on the ring I'd selected for her. Tears formed like diamonds on her cheeks and I wondered if everyone had noticed. What a dearly beloved! She'll make an excellent wife. I'm so miserable that I'm here, and she's miles away; I wish she were here now. The cook sat in his room and looked over the cookbook and his raise and Winchester. In the bunkhouse, all was serene. A couple cowboys were singing and others were humming *Silent Night*. Finally, the room began to cool down and wool blankets were pulled up to their throats, and a very happy group of cowboys fell off to sleep.

"Yes, sir. That was the best Christmas I ever had," said one in a low voice.

"Thank you, Lord," grinned one, as he went to sleep.

DIVIDING MY FORCES

A week into the new year of 1866, I dressed early that morning so that I might catch Paul and Rex before they got started branding cattle. We'd been branding cattle since two days after Christmas.

"I'm going to give you guys an option. I want to send one of you west with the hundred head of horses, and the other I want to stay here and get these cattle branded," I said.

"I'll take the horses," said Paul. "Rex might get lost, and besides, that's Comanche and Kiowa territory around the grasslands, and those dog soldiers would love to have his black hair decorating their wigwam."

"I'm satisfied just to stay right here," said Rex.

"Okay, Paul it is," I said. "Paul, I want you to make sure that you've a bill of sale for each horse, and make sure the bill of sale describes the right horse. The army will brand their horses. Paul, bridle the lead horses, and I believe that the others will follow. Don't let some wild stallion run off with the mares. Post a couple of guards every night as every Comanche and Kiowa will try to steal as many as they can. Take the pack mules and carry ample supplies, but be careful, and don't lose those bills of sale. I want you to bring back the amount of twelve thousand five hundred dollars in greenbacks. Those are prime horses, and broke to ride. I'll be looking to see you back here in five to six weeks. Take half of the men with you, and take your Winchesters. Remember, every horse you lose will cost me a hundred twenty-five dollars. Take the rest of the day to gather the horses, and select the right bills of sale. The cook will help you to estimate and pack the food on the mules.

Good luck, Paul, and take a dozen extra horses in case you lose a few, and take two riding horses for each man," I said.

"Do you know where Fort Craig is? It's one of the largest forts in the West and was constructed to help put down Indian uprisings in 1854. I understand it covers forty acres and has adobe walls. I've heard that it had a garrison of four thousand troops at one time. It's about two hundred sixty miles from here, and it should take about two weeks to get there and two weeks to get back. The terrain isn't bad, so you should make good time. I want you to leave as soon as possible, and be back here by the first of March."

"Rex, round up as many cows and bulls as you can. There're plenty of year-old bulls that need to be altered and branded. Brand as many young heifers as you find. Branding those old mossy fellows is out of the question. I don't want anyone hurt or busted up. The cold weather should keep the flies off, so I want at least fifty branded a day. It's hard work, but it has got to be done. Divide your men into teams of two or three to a team. Keep the herd watered and well-fed, and I want them to put on some weight before we start our drive to the fort," I instructed.

"I knew that I would have my work cut out for me," Rex said.

TROUBLE AT THE
LINE SHACKS!

The second month into branding, I thought I'd ride up toward the Colorado River and look for the three line cabins that were supposed to be near the river. I had the cook pack food for a three-day trip, and took a canteen of water and my grulla mare. Jane hadn't been ridden for a few days and appeared to be eager for the exercise. About a mile from the river, I saw one of the cabins and scouted it carefully just in case some Kiowa might be living there. The house appeared to be vacant, so I rode in. The door was tightly closed, and I found a skeleton key stuck in the lock. Someone had been there, but we tried to keep food in the pantry just in case someone riding through might have an emergency and need to lay up for a few days.

Out by myself, I was very careful to keep watch for Indians. I tied my horse to a tree and climbed the steps to the porch. From there, I had an excellent view of the river valley and saw a large herd of sixty or seventy wild horses drinking water at the river. They were mostly mustangs, but there was a beautiful black stallion. I saw several deer and antelope grazing in the grasslands. The grass had been burned some from the snow storm, but I saw no dead cattle. I rode on to the next house.

The second line shack had a large barn that we'd filled with hay last summer. Several head of cattle had taken refuge in the barn, and had remained there through the snow storm. From the house, I counted close to five hundred head of cattle in the waist-high grass. Don had left all of his cattle, as he said he would. If I could find a market for them, I would have an excellent commodity for income. No one had bothered the dwelling, so I rode on to the last line shack.

The third and last had occupants. I watched a man and woman moving around the house. Smoke curled upward from the chimney. The woman spotted me as I rode toward the house, and called a warning, and the man ran for his rifle.

"Stop right there, mister," he said, and pointed his rifle at me.

I kept my hands away from my gun, and I asked him if I could come up.

"What do you want?" he asked.

"I'm Tom McDowell," I said. "You're living in my cabin. This is one of my line shacks and you'll have to vacate it. I don't mind you staying for a few days, but the food and the wood you'll need to replenish."

"I'm George Montgomery, and this is my wife, Erma. I just got out of the army. My wife and I've been on the road for two months. We're from Southern Indiana. I fit with the Indiana 13th Battery of Light Artillery. Since we won the war, I'm claiming this land as my own. I was told when I signed up in 1861 I'd be given land when the war was over. This valley is mighty pretty, and I claim her as mine. You got whipped and we'uns are taking over."

"Now, Mr. Montgomery, the war is over and we're back home. I've a very old deed for this land, and you'll not claim this as your own. You're in a house that belongs to the TM Ranch. I own this land, as I paid cash for it. I'll give you a week to leave. Also, there are some Kiowa, Comanche, and Apache in this area, and they're savages. They'll kill you and steal your woman if you're not careful. Remember, you must be out within a week," I said as earnestly as I could.

I sat on my horse about twenty-five yards away, with my Winchester across my lap. He looked at me in a menacing manner and held his rifle at the ready as I'd seen northern troopers do.

"George," said Erma. "We can't steal his land like that."

"Hush, Erma!" he bellowed, and followed his words with a line of profanity. "You keep your mouth shut," he shouted at her.

"Mr. McDowell, you're not going to run us out of here. We've squatter's rights. Now you back away, and don't lift your rifle at me or mine. I won this place when I fit in the army."

Now what? I wondered. *Would there be other Northern troopers that would come to claim my land?* I backed my mare and held my Winchester ready. I didn't want to cause him bodily harm, but I didn't want him on my place either. It's a draw, for the time being. I began to get angry and felt the man was illiterate; maybe he really thought he was in the right. I wish the Yankee army was here to settle this dispute.

"Remember, Mr. Montgomery, you've got one week."

I felt that if I turned my back to him, he'd shoot me, so I continued to back my mare and watched him carefully.

•

On my way back to the ranch, I saw several more wild horses. I wondered how I could trap them so that we could break them. Horses had utility, but the cattle had no market. Now I had another problem: what to do with Montgomery. I considered calling the law; I was sure that it'd fall under the Texas Ranger authority. But it could be a federal problem too. I'd abide by the law, and I'd be happy if that young lieutenant came to straighten it out.

While out in the grasslands, the clouds gathered and I could not see the sun. Texas is a big place, and in those grasslands, everything looked the same, especially when it was overcast and you couldn't see the sun. I found it easy to get turned around, and wondered if I was moving south or west. I took out my compass, and found that I'd turned north again, when I should've been going southeast. My thoughts went back to a patrol during the war, when our unit captured some Yankee supplies. While my men were looking for food, I'd found a carton of twelve compasses and had issued them to officers under me as well as my non-commissioned officers. I kept them when I was promoted, and still had them at the war's end. I almost threw them away at Appomattox, but carried them on home and had them in my office now at the ranch.

When I arrived back at the ranch, I issued a compass to several of my cowboys, and took time to explain how the compass worked.

I also told them about the lay of the land, and when the sun was out, a person wouldn't have any difficulty, but could easily get lost on a cloudy day.

"When you leave here and head into the grassland area, carry a compass."

It brought smiles to all the men as they thought of their boss being completely turned around, but then they got rather serious when they remembered they'd been in similar straits.

"I don't have one of these for all of you, so go when you can be with someone who has one. We'll leave one at the bunkhouse, where Rex can keep track of it," I stated.

I wrote a letter to Matt and explained the situation with Mr. Montgomery. I wanted it handled correctly, to avoid trouble between the ranch and any possible reconstruction problems. I'd heard that union soldiers had been promised lands as compensation for their time in the service.

"Rex, I want you to pick out someone to carry a letter to the ranger for me. Whoever goes, please wait for an answer," I instructed.

Slim Wilkins, who was working with me to teach me the fast draw, volunteered to go "to get away for a day." He passed Paul returning from the south after delivering the horses and should've been coming out of the north. Slim joked with Paul and told him that I'd been turned around also.

"I wanted to see Melody anyway," joked Paul. "I only went ten hours out of the way to see her."

Slim showed Paul the compass. "That gadget would keep me out of town," Paul quipped.

The cook was somewhat put out, as the returning crew didn't get home in time for dinner. He was happy to see them all back and began to prepare another meal. Paul handed me a draft in the amount of $12,500. They'd been gone for two months.

"Have any trouble?" I asked.

"Yep, had some problems with young bucks trying to steal our horses one night, but Jimmy was on guard and wide awake. Boss, he earned his sixty dollars a month that night. Those new Winchesters can sure be discouraging to horse thieves," he smiled.

"We were all wide awake when Jimmy started shooting and gave him some help. We killed five braves and the horses didn't get out of their rope corral. We were lucky!"

"The army was extremely happy with the horses and I've an order for another hundred head, to be delivered in June. I asked the major if we could deliver some mustangs. He looked skeptical, but said he'd send a detail over here to look at them the first of June. He'd pay up to a hundred each for the mustangs if they're broken," declared Paul.

My thoughts went immediately to the wild horses that I'd seen near the river. *If I can get Mr. Montgomery out of that line shack and move my crew into those three houses, we could see how many of those mustangs we could rope, corral, and break to the saddle before the first of June.*

"Got lost coming home 'cause I didn't want to run into the tribe that tried to steal our horses; I'm sure they are angry at us for killing so many of them. I went farther south and came into Big Spring from the west. It took me an extra day, but we still have our scalps," Paul confessed, and I nodded in agreement.

•

Slim came in the next day with Matt's answer to the letter regarding Montgomery. Matt said he'd telegraph the army and should have an answer in a day or two. It sounded to him like it was a ticklish situation, and that the army ought to handle it. Bess and Delight sent their love. Slim also carried a sealed letter from Delight.

Delight said how she'd enjoyed the Christmas party and that her mother and dad were thrilled with their gifts. Matt especially enjoyed the Appaloosa. She looked forward to May 10th. She'd seen Paul at the restaurant visiting Melody on his way home from a horse delivery. Delight said that she'd spent some time with Melody, and got to know her better. Melody had become a close friend, and Delight was thinking of asking her to be maid of honor at the wedding. "I believe," wrote Delight, "that Melody is in love with Paul, and he seemed the same with Melody." Delight sent all her love.

I put her letter down and felt a desire to see her and hold her in my arms. May 10th was nearly three and a half months away. I was sure sorry that I doubted her and wished she was here now. I'd made a decision to be hesitant about our marriage, and here I am, miserable, for she was in town and I was out here.

MUSTANG HUNTING

I took my cowboys away from branding and headed north to scout out the land around the line shacks in order to start breaking the wild mustangs. The mustang is a stout animal and much prized, especially by the Indians. The Indian had captured the wild horse and, with only a blanket and a piece of raw hide for a saddle, had ridden circles around the army. The Indian would ride the mustang until the horse collapsed, and then would kill and eat the creature. The mustang knew little about love and, being highly spirited, would try to show the rider just who was boss. Many an Indian, though expert in riding, was pitched ungracefully to the ground. Three of my cowboys owned mustangs as their private horses, and told me how fond they were of mustangs. Before we left the ranch, I showed my crew on my map the approximate locations of the houses. A few of the cowboys had been there last summer and filled the barns with hay, but this was a strange area to most of them. I wanted the entire crew to know where the high ridges were, for Montgomery might scale those ridges to be watching for us. Since his time to vacate the house was up, I felt certain that he'd be watching for us with rifle in hand.

The Mexicans had a well-defined trail leading northwest to the line shack that Montgomery had inhabited. The grass was so high along the trail, that if you were twenty yards from the trail, you might not be able to see it. The trail wound between some very low hills, and the higher ridges would be places that we must watch in order to ride into the area unobserved. I stopped my crew and told them to stay on the trail and asked Paul and Rex to follow me on foot so I could point out some high ridges to them.

We moved through the waist-high grass, as I showed Paul and Rex how I wanted them to advance with their men on both sides of the trail. If there was no one on the ridges; then I wanted them to observe the house for signs of life. It may be that Montgomery and his wife were gone.

The cook, with the chuck wagon, was to remain in the trail until we called him to bring up the supplies. I saw to my right, near the top of the ridge, several circling buzzards, which I pointed out to Paul and Rex. Paul and Rex went back to direct the two-pronged advance and I decided to check out what was the reason for the circling buzzards. Lying on his back near the top of the highest hill was the stiff body of Mr. Montgomery. He'd been shot twice by arrows, and the Indian didn't want to lose his arrows, so he'd cut them out with his knife. The Indian had scalped Mr. Montgomery and terribly mutilated his body. The buzzards were at work on Montgomery's body and had pulled out his intestines, and one was pulling at them when I waved them away. I'd heard that the Apache mutilated when they killed, and here was proof to me.

I saw movement higher up on the ridge, and Paul and his crew melted into the grass. On the other ridge, where Rex was advancing, there was a burst of Winchester fire. The gunfire died out as quickly as it began.

Rex called to me, "Tom, Apaches over here! They're using bow and arrows. We've killed a half breed," he cried. "I saw three more running down the far side of the ridge."

From the top of the ridge, we looked down on the line shack that Mr. Montgomery had occupied. I could still see his covered wagon at the edge of the barn and wondered where Mrs. Montgomery was. Cautiously, we advanced on the house. The door opened slightly, and the nose of a shotgun protruded.

"Please don't come any nearer, or I'll shoot," she said.

I breathed a sigh of relief upon finding her still alive.

"Don't shoot, Mrs. Montgomery! We're the TM crew, and we just exchanged shots with a band of Apaches," I said.

Mrs. Montgomery stepped out onto the porch.

"Thank God!" she said on recognizing me. "Have you seen my husband?"

"I'm sorry, Mrs. Montgomery, but we did find him, and he's been dead for some time. His body is up there on the ridge. He'd been shot in the back with an arrow," I said.

Mrs. Montgomery sat down on the porch and placed her head in her hands as she wept.

"Two days ago, my husband brought four men into the house who appeared to be half breed Indians. One had a scar on his cheek and had a bad left arm, which he could use only partially," she said.

"Juan Garcia," I said. "You're lucky to be alive. He had a few of his friends up there on the ridge with him."

"I felt something had happened to my husband. He told this Mr. Garcia about your being here and they took him to the top of the ridge to watch for you on the trail. They were drinking my husband's wine, and I became concerned about him when, about sunset, the four Indians approached the house and my husband wasn't with them. I'd locked the door and told them to go away until my husband came to the door with them. They tried to force the door open and heard me load the shotgun and pull back both hammers. They didn't try to come in then."

She sat on the porch with her face in her hands and said, "Now what am I going to do?"

"We're sorry about your husband, and we'll fetch his body as soon as we can make sure there're no more Indians around. If you want, we can bury him down here or up there on the ridge."

"Please bury him on the ridge, for I don't want to see him dead." She wept some more. "The war ruined him; he was a good man until he went off to war and came back a drunken animal."

"Rex, take a couple of men up there and bury what's left of him." I spoke so she'd not hear. She sure didn't need to see his body in that condition. "Paul, send someone to tell the cook to bring up the chuck wagon," I continued.

I turned to Mrs. Montgomery and said, "We'll be in the line shacks for a week or two while we look for wild horses. We'll take you back to the ranch when we go home. If you'd like to help the cook, please feel free to do so. You can stay in this house and no one'll bother you. There'll be three or four of our crew that'll sleep in this front room, and you can have the back room. One or two can sleep in the loft until we scout this area," I said. "The Apache may well come back with extra warriors."

"My George told me that this area was full of wild horses, deer, and cattle that aren't branded," volunteered Mrs. Montgomery.

I thought of some of the wild horses that I'd seen; that black stallion was still on my mind.

"Rex, take your crew in the morning and see if those two other line shacks are inhabited. Look out for Garcia and the Apaches. Take some supplies with you for food, and carry canned goods to restock the line shacks. Paul, send out patrols and see if the Apache are still around. That Juan is a mean, murderous cutthroat, so watch out for him. He has three half breeds with him. If you can see that they're cleared out of this area, let's look for those wild horses. Try to count the horses you see, and cattle too, so we might get an estimate on what's here. Use those compasses if you need to, but all the rivers run from northwest toward the southeast, which should be helpful," I said.

•

We scouted the area for several days, and found deer, antelope, cattle, and hundreds of wild horses. One evening, Rex came to me and said, "Tom, I believe I know how to catch those horses. They're using a box canyon on the other side of the west ridge. I thought it had no exit until I saw how they got out at the western end. If we could roll down some rocks and block the western exit, the box canyon could be closed and we'd have whatever was in it. When a herd enters the canyon, we could throw up a fence across the eastern entrance and snare the whole herd."

"Show me."

We climbed to the rim of the box canyon and watched several herds pass through the canyon.

"That's our answer," I agreed. "There's a good five hundred horses using this area. I'd like to get half of them. We can hold them in the box canyon until we break them and build a corral to retain the ones that are broken. I believe we can fill our order for the army in a matter of three months right here."

"We need to post a couple guards and keep an eye open for Indians," said Paul.

Mrs. Montgomery insisted on helping the cook, and the cowboys treated her with respect. She tried to mother all of them and soon became a very special lady to them. Her presence helped soften their vocabulary, as they refrained from telling lewd stories and using profanity. I insisted that prayer be made for the food, and told them how I'd found a need to pray. I was full of thanksgiving that I'd come through the war untouched. Some of the cowboys also had stories of nearly being killed in the war.

The work was difficult, but I worked as hard as the others. March came and I sent word to Matt that the trouble at the line shack had been corrected and told him of the death of Mr. Montgomery. I also mentioned that Mrs. Montgomery had seen Juan Garcia and we'd killed one of Juan's men.

We were in our third week of March when we were surprised to see a Yankee patrol come up the trail, and Matt was with them. Mrs. Montgomery was asked to tell about the death of her husband, and why they'd inhabited the line shack. The lieutenant asked me if I'd heard of the Thirteenth Amendment to the Constitution or of the Freedmen's Bureau.

"Yes, sir, I have, but the situation involving Mr. Montgomery didn't apply. This land wasn't abandoned land, nor was Mr. Montgomery a slave, nor was he a "refugee," having been driven from his home because of his loyalty to the north. I don't believe this land was assigned to him. He just took it without a cause," I replied.

The lieutenant agreed.

He saw the black stallion and his herd, and decided that the army would take the mustangs. Scouts from the army were sent off to try to find the Apache, but it was futile. All wondered why the Apache were back in this area.

I wonder if Juan Garcia stirred them up and wanted them to become involved in his revenge against me, I speculated.

When the patrol was about to leave, they asked Mrs. Montgomery if she wanted to go with them. She approached me and told me she had no home or anywhere to go. I held her in my arms and told her she had a home at the hacienda. She could be a maid to help Delight when we married in May. This really pleased her, and she told the lieutenant she'd been offered work and would remain with us at the line shacks to cook and mend for the TM Ranch.

I held up the patrol while I wrote a note to Delight to send by Matt. In my note, I told Delight that I had hired Mrs. Erma Montgomery and asked if she minded having a maid and house-keeper at the hacienda. I told her about Erma not having a home, and how all the cowboys loved her and appreciated her. I'd let her stay at the hacienda and would assign her a room off the kitchen, with the understanding that the room was a temporary setup.

Delight, I want you to run the hacienda and assign who sleeps where, I wrote.

I felt what I said would please her, and she would appreciate my thinking. Matt took the note to Delight.

With Matt and the troopers gone, I assigned two of my men to scout out the area. I didn't know what the Kiowa or the Comanche thought of our being here. All three tribes were residents of this area, and all were basically of the same family. The Apache dwelt more in the desert areas of New Mexico than in this grassy plain.

I set the men to making a portable fence and gate that could be carried into place once the horses had entered the box canyon. The fence was massive and would require at least ten men to get it in place. The poles were made from pine trees that were near the river. We used cedar and locust wood for the fence posts. I decided that the rocks would be rolled to block the western section, or what we thought of as the rear of the box canyon, toward the end of the day. The horses usually entered the canyon during the night. Several large rocks were sent crashing into the canyon, and Rex called from the floor of the canyon.

"The exit is sealed."

"We did it. I don't think a goat can climb out this back way," said Paul, as we laid along the rim of the canyon, careful to be down-wind from the herd, and watched for the horses.

"I don't think that black stallion is in there yet. I believe most of the herd is just west of the entrance to the canyon," he continued.

Rex had climbed out of the canyon and joined us on the lip of the rim.

"Look at all those horses," he whispered. "Boss, do you think we could drive the rest of them in?"

"Yes. If we get that black stallion moving, the rest will follow," I whispered. "There he is now! He's lifting his head, smart horse, and very alert. I think he smells where you've been, Rex. Don't move. There, he's going in. Told you he'd lead them in, for it looks like most of them are following now," I said with excitement. "Rex, Paul, hurry and put up that fence and gate. Boy, have we got a bunch of horses," I added, grinning.

The cowboys were tugging on the fence and gate. Four rode their horses between the wild horses and the gate, and the horses went deeper into the canyon. The black stallion was whistling and stamping his hoofs, and the herd was very restless.

"You fellows on the horses try to keep the herd away from the fence and gates till those post holes are fully tamped. Great job, guys!" I yelled.

"That was a good day's work, and I think we got all of them; at least, that stallion's entire herd," Paul said. "Boy, I'm worn out."

"Four of you men stay here at the fence, and make sure the herd doesn't press on our fence and try to overrun it. The rest of you, go back to the house and get some sleep. Paul and Rex, divide the men equally so all get the same amount of sleep. Good night, men!" I called.

•

I went to the lip of the canyon early the next morning after break-fast. Paul was counting the horses he could see in the canyon. He had a pencil and pad, and was adding figures.

"They're not fully settled down yet, but several are lying exhausted there by the stream. Look at that black stallion prance! He's been whistling and tried going over the rocks twice since I've been here. I've counted 195 twice, but I might've missed a couple back in the shade there. There are some beautiful horses down there, and they're in their winter coats. They'll look a lot better this summer when they've shed, and we can clean them up. I believe we can get the one hundred dollars each for a little more than half, and the rest should bring one hundred twenty-five," Paul said.

All that talk told me that Paul was excited, for he was a man of few words.

"I want you to pick out twenty good horses for our own use, and brand them. Break them, and when you are satisfied that they're well broken, I want you to train them to be cow ponies. I've an idea that we'll need good cattle ponies with all the cattle that needs to be branded yet. There's got to be a market for beef," I said to Paul. "And Paul, save that black stallion, and don't put a brand on him."

"Well, the fun is over and the work has begun," drawled Rex.

We cut and made cedar posts; pine trees were used for the fencing, and we constructed a sturdy corral. We broke the horses to bridle and bit, and then came the saddle blanket, followed by the saddle. There were five of our cowboys that boasted there wasn't a four-legged critter they couldn't ride. By the end of the second day, all five were so sore that they limped about camp moaning. All twelve of the cowboys got their opportunity to ride. Rex would hold the head of the pony and bite the ponies' ear until the rider was well-settled in the saddle. The horse exploded into activity, and many a cowboy was pitched over the head of the mustang. The cowboys were in stiff competition of who could ride the most ornery mustang.

VISIT FROM THE KIOWA

I sent five men back to the ranch and rotated them so that all the men, including me, had some rest from the grueling task of breaking mustangs. We'd worked for two weeks, when one morning, one of the scouts came riding to the canyon.

"Hey, Boss! Indians!" he yelled, and pointed to a cloud of dust to the north. All the cowboys ran to their horses for their Winchesters. They opened boxes of cartridges from their saddlebags and checked each gun to make sure they were fully loaded. They stood near some large rocks and watched the approaching Indians.

Rex came over to me and said, "I remember that chief. Don traded with him. The chief speaks Spanish, and I remember some. He is holding his hand up in a gesture of peace."

There were about fifty braves in the group, but there was no war paint, so I told my boys to let them come in. The braves looked a little uneasy as they saw each cowboy had a repeating rifle. I stepped forward and raised my hand, to show that I wanted peace. The old chief was looking around our camp. We had gathered about twenty head of cattle to fatten and hold for our cook. We had two corrals with horses in them. One group was branded, and the other was not. The unbranded group were good-looking mustangs, about twenty-five in number. Rex spoke to the old chief in Spanish and was answered in Spanish, amid a few Kiowa words and hand gestures.

Rex said to me, "He says his name is Wolf Fang, and the Apache calls you 'Straight Shooter with a Gun.' He says that you can shoot straight. Boss, that day when you killed those Apaches may well be what he speaks of. He wants to smoke the peace pipe with you."

"Tell him to come into the shade, and let's get some of that rum tobacco in my saddlebag to smoke, and some for a gift," I replied.

The chief brought out several deerskin jackets. He waved his hand at them, as he told Rex they were gifts for me. Rex thanked him and turned to me.

"He wants some of the horses and the cattle we have penned up."

"The horses in that one corral have been branded and will be sore for a while," I said.

Rex spoke to the Chief and the old chief looked at the branded ponies.

"The beautiful horses in the other corral, I'll give to you, along with all the cattle in the holding pen," I said.

"Good, it's a trade," said Rex, "and he is pleased with the trade."

"Straight Shooter, good friend," said the Chief in English.

"Wolf Fang is good friend," I replied.

I had traded twenty-five unbroken mustangs for five deerskin jackets.

Wolf Fang then turned to his braves and spoke to them in the Kiowa language. The braves uttered a few cries as the cowboys opened the corrals. The Indians moved in, and the mustangs were brought out. The cattle were moved out of their corral, and they all moved toward the north. The five cowboys who said they could ride anything burst out laughing. They laughed so hard that one rolled on the ground. The others would've done the same, but they were all beat up from trying to break the twenty-five horses that the Indians were taking home.

"Ha! Ha! Ha!" yelled one of the five. "We'd all given up on that group. We were wondering just what we could do with them. None of us could ride them. Ha! Ha! Ha! There'll be some sore Indian braves in that tribe before this week is over. I wonder if they'll kill and eat them."

"Rex," I said. "How do you think that Kiowa chief knew about my fight with the Apache?"

"Boss, that land to the north is called Indian Territory, and there're Comanche, Apache, and Kiowa tribes living in that area. The Comanche and the Apache come from the same family background. All three tribes live in this area and north of the ranch," Rex said. "What a Kiowa hears from his intermingling with other tribes, he brings to his chief. Old Wolf Fang knows what goes on in those Indian lands."

I was impressed that Rex knew so much about Indians, but Don was a sharp old Mexican and got along well with the various tribes.

"Rex, if you see any way that I can be friendly and live in peace with these Indians, please let me know," I remarked.

We still had a couple of hours left to work, so I sent the cowboys back to breaking mustangs.

•

April came, and I continued rotating my cowboys to work at the ranch. The five who stayed at the ranch watched over the property and fed stock, both horse and cattle. They also branded cattle and altered some of the young bulls, as well as branded heifers. I brought back to the ranch eighty head of broken horses and took my turn at the ranch. I brought the cook with me and left Erma to cook for the wranglers. We made more corrals, and I began a project of building a large horse barn with several stalls and an area for hay storage in the loft. I sent one of my wranglers into town and had Matt send out a good carpenter to do the main carpentry for us. He was a Mormon and very religious, but I told him that I didn't believe his doctrine. He stopped trying to win me to his religion when I read to him from Galatians 1:1–9. We never discussed religion afterwards.

April slowly crawled by and then May was finally here. The barn was ninety percent finished, and the corrals were full of horses. Branded cattle dotted the countryside. It was clear that I'd have to wait till after the wedding to deliver the one thousand head of cattle. Spring was displaying its beauty; the fields were full of wildflowers, and the trees were in bloom. I exchanged the cook for Erma, and she came to the ranch to clean, and prepare her own room off the kitchen. Her room was large and had a nice window. All the windows had shutters with rifle port holes. Don had not only built a lovely home, but a fort as well.

On the fifth of May, all the wranglers brought the remaining horses to TM. The horse barn was full, and the new corrals were filled with horses. The branded cattle were running wild and dotted the fields. The bunkhouse, barns, well house, and blacksmith shop were all given a new coat of whitewash. The hacienda was whitewashed last. The flower gardens around the hacienda were weeded and the place looked like paradise itself. The apple trees and peach trees were blooming, and small fruit had appeared.

•

On the eighth of May, Matt, Bess, Delight, and Melody arrived in the surrey. Delight was simply beautiful with rosy cheeks and her blond hair piled high on her head. Her green eyes were sparkling, and her dimple was deep as she looked with pleasure on the TM Ranch. I threw my arms around her and kissed her on the lips several times, and then I gave a big hug to Bess, kissed her on her cheek. I introduced them all to Erma, and everyone found Erma as friendly and nice as I said she was.

OUR MARRIAGE DAY

Paul was there to take Melody away for a while. I asked Matt when the preacher was planning to come, and he said the preacher was coming with some guests from town. Paul was to be the best man, and Rex and two cowboys, Slim Wilkins and Roy Jenkins, were ushers. Slim and Roy had won the honor by drawing high cards, for I didn't want to show favoritism.

A pianist from the church in town played the grand piano in the parlor, and with the windows opened, the music could be heard. Matt would give his daughter in marriage. The carpenter had constructed a frame canopy, and flowers from the garden were cut and placed over it. The ceremony would be conducted under the canopy, and the guests would sit facing the canopy. The cook and Erma had baked a large wedding cake, and a huge table was set up to serve the meal.

Extra bunks were placed in the bunkhouse for male guests that would stay overnight. The day before the wedding, all participating guests had arrived, and a practice session went along smoothly. Food was served, and everything was prepared to the last detail.

I awoke nervous, for it was our wedding day. The girls giggled and fussed that I wasn't to see Delight before the wedding. I went to the barn and ran into the cowboys. They kidded me unmercifully, and I told Paul that we might as well make it a double wedding. The cowboys switched their kidding to him, and I sort'a got away from them at Paul's expense.

Matt was having trouble tying his tie.

"You'd better get ready, *son*," he said, grinning.

The pianist began to play, and Paul and I walked around the

hacienda to approach the canopy from the right side. Matt went into the house to take his daughter's arm and lead her to the altar. Paul and I and the ushers all marched ahead and waited at the altar as the wedding march was played. Melody was dressed in a pink full dress, which Delight's mother had made; her blue eyes were radiant, and her brown hair accentuated her beauty. The pianist hit the chords and everyone stood, and I looked up the aisle to Matt and the most beautiful girl that I'd ever seen. A veil partially covered her face, her gown flowed along her back, and her train moved gently behind her. We said our vows to one another, and I placed my ring on her finger. Melody took the flowers that Delight had in her arms, and Delight tilted her face to receive my kiss; and Delight was my wife.

We had several beautiful gifts given to us by well-wishers, and we had fun eating and serving one another the cake. We ate an excellent meal, and the guests began to leave. The marriage had been set for two in the afternoon so that those attending could ride back home before it got too late to see. Matt, Bess, and Melody all promised that they'd return soon. Paul rode his horse and followed the surrey as Matt and Bess and Melody rode for town.

The cowboys all lined up to kiss the bride and then dismissed themselves early and quietly retired to the bunkhouse. Some had met old girlfriends that they'd not seen for a while, and rode back to town with them to protect them.

Delight was timid and shy as we consummated our marriage, and we were now one in body. I belonged to her, and she belonged to me. We were one.

The sun of a new day came peeping through the window at me, and I slipped out of bed and watched her sleep. I'm not one to lie in bed, so I dressed quietly and went to the bunkhouse. I planned to outline the work for the day. The carpenter was already busy tearing down the canopy.

"Congratulations," said Rex. "You know, Paul's not in yet. How in the world could a girl like Melody love him when I'm here?" He shook his head in disbelief, smiling all the while.

Erma and the cook had made breakfast for us, but Delight didn't get up and I ate alone. I would let her sleep. At 8:30, I slipped into our bedroom and she heard me enter. She held out her arms to me and I kissed her. What a beautiful woman she was!

"Hmmmm! I love that!" She smiled. "Come on back to bed. This is our honeymoon, you know."

I quickly complied with her request.

The week moved right along, and we enjoyed one another. I thanked Him every day for his goodness to me, and the happiness that was ours. I remembered at the battle of the Wilderness how I'd raised my head over the trench to see if the enemy was advancing. A Minié ball cut a notch in my hat, and I heard the gun report across the woods. Quickly, I pulled my head down, and right then I said a prayer ,as was my custom.

"I thank you, Lord, for sparing my life."

"Delight," I said. "I'd like to have devotions every day with you. I came through the war and had so many close calls that I feel blessed, oh, so blessed. You're my wife, and I love you! How truly blessed I am! Will you pray with me?"

She agreed, and it became a habit in our young lives.

•

It was after a week of bliss that I decided to get back to work. The cowboys had been busy branding all the cattle, and the horses that we were going to keep. The hundred head of mustangs we didn't brand would be branded by the U.S. army. We needed to send a wire to the fort to see if they were ready for delivery. I took Delight into town with me so she could visit with her parents while I wired the fort in New Mexico. I let her ride my grulla horse, for I knew the mare was gentle. I decided to ride the black stallion which I named "Ebony," as he was solid black. I had ridden him around the ranch several days, and I fed and showed affection to him. He seemed so intelligent that I thought he might know what I was saying when I spoke affectionately to him. We made the trip without mishap, and Matt and Bess were very pleased to see us; we shared Delight's old room.

I HIRE A SCOUT

"Matt, I *need* someone who can scout for me on some of these horse deliveries. Know of anyone I can hire who knows New Mexico?"

"Tom, as a matter of fact, I do. We've a man that was on the expedition with General Stephen Watts Kearny when he took New Mexico without firing a shot. General Kearny had been told by General Winfield Scott at Craig's Fort to recruit some Missourians who were in caravans heading toward California. That was back during the Mexican War, around 1846, about twenty years ago, when Amos DeJohn was twenty years old. I'd say that he's forty now. He told me that General Kearny recruited about four or five companies of Mormons along with the Missourians. There were three thousand Mexicans lying in wait for the Americans, and you know General Kearny sort of talked them out of it. He went right on and captured Santa Fe. Anyway, Amos went with Kearny and really got to know most of New Mexico. He'd make a good scout, I believe. Usually forty would be old, but Amos is a tough customer," Matt said.

"Tom, there's something else I'd try to find out if I were you. Charles Bent, who was from Taos, was appointed territorial governor by General Kearny. While governor, Bent signed several treaties with the Indians. I'd try to find how the Indians are staying true to the treaty, and which tribes signed," Matt said.

I agreed that was a good idea.

"Is this Amos DeJohn around here these days?" I asked.

"Let's try a saloon or two. He drinks some, but nothing too bad," answered Matt. "I saw him just day before yesterday, and he lives on the outskirts of town. This time of day, he should be in one of these saloons." Matt looked over the swinging doorway bats of one of the three saloons in town. "Don't see him in there."

The second saloon was approached in the same manner.

"There he is," said Matt. I followed Matt into the Last Chance Saloon, which was near the edge of town, and apparently not far from Amos DeJohn's home.

Amos was a short man with long hair, and he had a black hat on his head. He wore buckskin clothing, and his blue eyes were fierce in the midst of a ruddy face. It was apparent that he had been drinking.

"Matt, you sure I want him?" I whispered.

"You won't have any trouble out of him once he's away from town," Matt whispered back.

Matt introduced us, and I must say, DeJohn held his liquor well. His eyes were bright, but he didn't stagger or slur his words.

"Mr. DeJohn," I said, "I own the TM Ranch, and I've contracted with the U.S. army to deliver some horses and cattle to Fort Craig in New Mexico. I have a few men who delivered horses there last winter, but they'd a run in with the Indians and had to fight to retain the horses. Some of the Indians were killed. I'm concerned that an Indian tribe will be laying for us this time. I'll be delivering a thousand head of cattle later on to the same fort, and could encounter the same problem."

"Tom, what would my job be? Is it a job as a scout that ye be offering me?" The accent was slightly Scottish. "I know that territory like the back of me hand. I was there originally with Kearny back in '46, and have been there many times to trade and look for silver in the mountains. I married a Kiowa girl from that area, and we go back to her people a couple times a yar," he said.

"Sounds good to me," I replied. "I'll pay $60 a month and supply a Winchester repeating rifle and shells."

"When do I start?" he asked.

"Can you be ready to go to the ranch, say, day after tomorrow?" I asked.

"Aye!" he replied.

"I'm staying with Matt at his house. I'm eating off my father-in-law," I said, smiling.

"You be one who married Delight then? Well, glad to meet you. I've known Matt and his family for twenty yars."

"Speaking of eating, I bet Bess has dinner waiting for us. We'd better move," Matt said.

We said good night to Amos and rode up the street.

"Matt, what Kiowa tribe did DeJohn marry into?" I asked.

"He married a chief's daughter. The old chief is Wolf Fang," said Matt.

I laughed in spite of myself and told Matt about the trade that we'd made.

"I've really wondered if they got that bunch of wild horses broken," I laughed.

"If you see him on this trip, don't tease him about that trade. How did the deerskin jackets turn out?" asked Matt.

"I've one on now," I answered. "His squaw sure knows how to condition deer skin. They chew the skins to soften them, so I've heard."

"I've been admiring your black horse, Tom. He is a very powerful animal and I bet he can run all day," Matt changed the subject.

"This is the first time that I've ridden him away from the ranch. This trip into town didn't seem to bother him, but I've been watching him around your Appaloosa. Delight tried to race me a time or two, but I held him back," I said. "Matt, what in the world do you want me to call you? Matt or Dad?"

"Well, Tom, I've never had a son and you can call me Dad if you want, or you can call me Matt," grinned Matt. "Tom, Delight seems especially happy and I'm pleased for you both."

We reached the house, and Matt rode to a small manger behind his back porch. Ebony whistled, and my mare replied. Matt's Appaloosa also whistled. We watered and fed all the horses and took off their saddles, blankets, and bridles.

"Matt, I'm going to buy a surrey tomorrow, and I'll see if I can have it delivered to the ranch. I saw a beauty in that harness shop next to the livery stable. I'll have one of the cowboys break a couple of horses to pull the rig, and then we'll bring it back here so you can bring Bess out to visit Delight. Delight only has Erma as a female companion, and she misses her mother. I'll be gone from the ranch the most of the next six to eight weeks. I'll leave ten of my cowboys at the ranch to protect Delight and care for cattle while I'm gone. Juan Garcia is still on the loose," I said.

"Tom, that's truly thoughtful of you, and I appreciate it very much," Matt said.

Dinner was waiting for us when we arrived, and I felt at home with Bess and Matt. I had no trouble calling them Mom and Dad. I'd never had a mother, and Bess truly mothered me and showed her love for me. Delight just beamed when I called her dad "Dad." Matt called on me to give thanks for the food and we held hands around the table as I prayed. They all said, "Amen!"

•

The next morning, I went to the harness shop and bought a red surrey with a beautiful tan roof and matching fringe. It had black steel wheels and tan steel rims. Since I'd no horse to pull it, I contracted with the livery man to deliver it to my ranch. He said he'd meet us at Matt's at six o'clock. We all had breakfast together, and when the livery man came with the surrey, everyone was delighted with the purchase. Bess and Delight tried out the leather seats, and the livery man drove them into town and back as we waited for DeJohn.

Amos arrived right on time and also admired the new surrey. I'd also purchased two new Winchesters with several cases of shells, which were in the backseat of the surrey. I took one of the Winchesters, loaded it, and gave Amos a rifle boot, which he attached to his saddle. He looked over the Winchester and raised it several times to his cheek and sighted down the gun. He dropped it into the boot and took several boxes of shells and put them in his saddlebags.

"Amos, the gun was made by Volcanic Arms Co., and was bought out by Winchester. People call them 'Yellow Boy' because of the brass receiver. They use Henry's 44 rim fire cartridges, and if you have a Colt 44 as I have, then the shells can be used in both guns," I said.

"Thank ye, mon," said Amos. "I've heard of the gun, but it's the first time that I've seen one. When we get outside of town, I want to see how it works, so I'll drop back so I won't spook the horses, if that's all right?"

"Sure!" I said.

We said good-bye to Matt and Bess and rode out of town, where Amos displayed some excellent shooting and smiled at the way the Winchester handled. He put the gun back into the boot and caught up with us.

The surrey was about twenty-five yards ahead of the three of us as we loped along the trail. It was beginning to get hot, as it was the last day of July. We spared our horses, as there wasn't reason for hurry. I sat on my horse between Amos and Delight and had gone about five miles from town when, suddenly, Amos yelled, "Lookout!" It was such a loud shout that the horses bolted. There was the whining of a bullet, and then the echo of a rifle shot; Amos had saved my life, for I felt the nearness of the passing bullet as it brushed my hair. I slapped the grulla on the rump and then reached for my Winchester. There was movement on a nearby hill, and both Amos and I fired. All three of our horses were moving rapidly along the trail. Amos and I turned toward the hill where the rifle had fired, and where we'd seen the movement. We saw dust, and then we saw riders, but they were now out of range. I saw a mustang standing, looking back toward the hill. The horse walked back and looked down into the grass.

Amos said, "We must have hit one of them. Be careful, for he may just be injured and not dead."

I approached the place where the horse stood, and there laid a half-breed face down in the grass. With my Colt revolver in my hand, I rolled him over and saw that he was dead. I called to the livery man and asked if he would report this shooting to Matt when he got back. I tied the Indian's mustang to the back of the surrey, and though he rebelled at first, he finally was willing to go along.

"That was a good shot, mon," said Amos. "I know that it wasn't me, lad, for I shot at movement higher on the ridge."

Delight was very nervous and alarmed at the incident. She rode along and didn't say a word, but watched the hills with frightened eyes. The rest of the ride home came without incident. The cowboys had seen us coming, and several rode out to meet us. They noticed that Amos was watching our back trail. When told that we'd been fired on, four of the cowboys suggested that they get some food and ride back to see if they might pick up the Apache's trail.

"It might lead into an ambush," I said, and Amos agreed. "I'll need everyone to get ready for the horse drive. This horse delivery might be the more dangerous of the two drives, for the Indians need horses, as does the army. Stealing horses, even between tribes, is done regularly and not considered a crime to them. We'll take ten cowboys, and since you've already been there, Paul, I want you to ramrod the outfit. Rex, because we had this encounter with Juan today, I want you to stay close to the ranch and guard the property, and especially watch out for Delight. Brand cattle, but stay near the ranch," I instructed.

"Paul, take an extra ten horses to be used by our crew, so we'll need one hundred twenty horses. Leave the grulla for Delight and Rex; watch Delight, and don't let her out of your sight. Cookie will come with us and Erma will cook here at the ranch. Cookie, take my two pack mules, and I believe that Paul knows a couple of those mustangs that'll carry the packsaddle. Any questions? There's a lot to do to get ready and we want to leave here in the morning so we can meet the army detail from Fort Craig. We've two weeks to get there," I said.

The crew began preparations for the trip. We'd move the horses west and ford the Rita Blanca. We'd be in Indian country and more so as we continued west. Amos would scout for us the best way to the fort and Paul would confer with the scouts each evening. Amos would look out for Indians, along with the two cowboys that'd scouted for several months when we broke the mustangs near the box canyon. I was disturbed about leaving Delight, and she tried to be cheerful and hide her worry, but she was concerned since the shooting on the trail. I told her not to ride out of sight of the ranch and to listen to Rex.

We were all ready at break of day and Amos and Paul led the horses toward the river to a place where Paul had forded before.

It was a beautiful morning, and after conferring with Paul, Amos and his two scouts rode ahead. The horse herd was causing a lot of dust that could be seen for many miles. Everyone was alert as we rode into New Mexico and turned northwest. Toward the middle of the day, we stopped near a small stream to water the horses. The scenery was mountainous and picturesque. Amos, followed by his scouts, came riding up in a bit of a hurry.

"We're being followed by a large band of Indians. I'm not sure if they are Kiowa or Comanche, but they're not Apache. They may well be concerned about us going through their territory," said Amos.

"Should I try to talk to them?" I asked. "I've some tobacco to give to their chief."

"They're following us right now and if they confront us, we might try diplomacy," said Paul, and Amos agreed.

"You know, on our first drive it was our second evening out that we had our trouble when those Indians tried to steal our horses. We're farther south than on our first drive. We killed several when they tried to raid us. I hope we're far enough south that it's not the same tribe," continued Paul.

"If they're the ones, lads, they'll appear with war paint on their faces," said Amos.

•

We camped near a stream that evening where we could run a rope corral from tree to tree. The horses were tired, as was my crew. Paul posted three guards and told them to be especially alert. I took a turn at guard duty at midnight. I knew little about the habits of the Kiowa, but knew them to be fierce warriors. I was very careful, and moved very little through my watch. I had taken off my Mexican spurs and replaced them with moccasins. Every night bird that called, I thought of the call as from a human throat. I knew where our other guards were and saw they were wide awake and as careful as I was. Our relief came at three o'clock. It would be light by five, and it was then that the attack might come, I reasoned. I was weary and needed some more sleep, but left word to awake me at five. I awoke to the smell of frying bacon and biscuits being cooked in a fireside oven. The cook was bending over a small fire and nodding toward me.

"Mornin,'" I said quietly.

"They're out there, Boss," the cook said. "Too many quail so near our camp. I can smell them and feel them in my bones."

The sun was just beginning to show pink in the eastern sky. I listened closely to a quail call. It was the call of an old hen, gathering her chicks to her as if they'd been scattered.

That may be the Indian war party's call to assemble for a rendezvous, I thought.

"Boss," called a guard, "there are eight bucks walking toward us from the west."

Everyone must have heard his remark, for our camp sprang to life. I heard a half dozen Winchesters being cocked and shells being pumped into the chambers.

"Paul, Amos, join me," I cried.

I saw the Indians standing warily and uncertain, and watching us closely. One had a breast plate of bones knit together across his chest and the skull of a wolf worn as a hat situated on his head. He lifted his hand as a gesture of peace.

"Tell them to come to our fire, Amos," I requested. Amos was speaking to them in Kiowa, and then he shifted to another dialect. I raised my arm as a sign of peace. They came to the fire, and since I saw no war paint, I believed them to be a hunting party.

"They are Pawnee, I think," said Amos. "That is Wolf Head, and a murderous old medicine man, he is," Amos spoke in English to us. "Don't look into the fire, men, as it will leave spots in front of your eyes and it'll be difficult to shoot," he continued. "See, the scalp locks are stiffened on the braves to stand up on their heads like curved horns. They are Pawnee, all right."

We had killed a deer and had some beef that I thought I might give the Indians. They appeared to be especially interested in the rum tobacco. I offered a bag of it to them, which they accepted greedily. The Indian with the wolf head spoke and appeared to be their leader.

"We want horses," he said bluntly, and Amos translated.

"Tell him no, Amos. Tell him that the horses belong to the white soldiers who made the treaty with the Indians when Wolf Head was young!"

Amos spoke and the Indian sat stiffly for a minute and reached for his spear. There was movement among the cowboys as a half dozen rifles came to bear on him. He threw the spear into the fire and without another word turned and left, followed by the other seven Indians.

Each cowboy grabbed some bacon and biscuits, and with bulging mouths, they lifted their saddles, saddle blankets, and bridles, and made for their horses. Others filled their canteens, while some stood with rifles and six-guns ready in case of an attack.

"What do you think?" I asked Paul and Amos. "I don't think that the young bucks think about the treaties much. They're interested in our horses, though, and I believe we might have to fight this bunch."

"They might attack this morning, or they may try to ambush us on the trail," said Amos. "The Pawnee have a name for being sneaky and cover themselves with wolf skin and lie in wait or attack at night."

"I agree. Be ready to fight," said Paul.

The sun made the eastern sky a little brighter and the cook cleaned his cooking tools and his oven was put into the stream to cool. I saddled Ebony and helped our crew take down the rope corral. We were ready to move, when a flight of arrows came showering down on us. They had been shot from a great distance and were not very accurate. One horse screamed and fell, pierced through with an arrow. With his rifle held a few inches from the animal's head, a cowboy pulled the trigger and the horse stopped screaming. We were out of sight, but the arrows kept coming.

Ebony lifted his head and whistled. There came an answer from a thicket to my right. Ten Indians riding at top speed came from the thicket, hanging onto their mounts with one leg while trying to fit their arrows to their bowstrings. They hid behind their horses and tried to keep their animals between them and us.

I lifted my rifle and my bullet went through the horses' neck and caught the Indian just below his nose. The warrior started to fall, but he had tied himself to his horse, and animal and rider both fell with a crash into the undergrowth. Other warriors were screaming their war cries and, seeing several of their tribe fall, began to back off. I was hoping one volley would be enough. We'd broken into an easy gait and managed to keep the herd together. I was concerned at the dust we were raising, for it could be seen for miles and the Indians knew exactly where we were. Amos and his two scouts laid down covering fire and positioned themselves between the herd and the Indians.

Roy Jenkins rode his horse near to me and shouted, "Boss, I've an arrow through my left thigh." Roy was one of the most popular cowboys in our crew. "That arrow sure was sharp as it went right through. The head of the arrow is on my inside thigh and I've lost blood."

I called for a halt, and the arrow was pulled on through the leg. I looked at the arrow head and smelled it. The arrow appeared to have been dipped in some animal or human manure. We bandaged his leg tightly and Roy said he thought he could ride on, but I knew his leg was giving him great pain. I motioned to one of the cowboys to ride by his side and watch him. Roy's leg hung down as he rode upright in the saddle, and I became more concerned for his welfare. The wound bled and continued to bleed. What we didn't realize, was that the arrow had pierced the main artery of his leg and he was bleeding internally. I saw that he was about to faint, and called a halt. His leg was turning purple, and the pain must have been terrible. Roy's face was very pale, and we stood over him and looked into his dying eyes. We were about to lose one of our own, and he was like a brother to us all. The cook lifted his head slightly and war-hardened men wrung their hats in their hands. No one had thought the wound was fatal or as severe as it was. He had ridden his horse without complaint, fearing for our safety if we stopped. Enduring the suffering, he smiled at us as if he was saying good-bye, and then he died. Tears were shed by hardened men and several tried not to reveal them and walked away so the tears couldn't be seen.

"Uncomplaining, Roy had tried to die without causing hardship to anyone," said Paul.

"We can't leave him here. Paul, tie him across his horse. We need to give him a Christian burial. Those Indians aren't far behind," I said, as I watched a dust cloud behind us.

Paul and others tied Roy across his horse and we were in the saddle again. Paul, Amos, and the two scouts set up an ambush and waited with Winchesters to discourage any future pursuit by the Indians; the rest pushed the horses. About a half hour later, we heard the rapid fire of the Winchesters and stopped to listen. By evening, we'd ridden forty miles, and Amos, Paul, and the scouts had rejoined us. We found a good camping place and washed most of the trail dust from our faces and arms. I sent three men to find a good burial place for Roy. They dug a grave beneath a cottonwood tree near the stream. While several cowboys joined together to share in the digging, the cook was busy preparing a meal. It was close to seven o'clock but, due to the time of the year, the sun had not set.

I took my Bible and, followed by my crew, carried Roy's body, which was wrapped in his blanket, down for his burial. The men stood with their hats in their hands and bowed their heads.

I read from the scriptures: "I am the resurrection and the life; he that believeth in me, though he were dead, yet shall he live: And whosoever liveth and believeth in me shall never die," John 11:25.

"Roy was a fine fellow, and though he was wounded, he didn't let us know how badly. That was the kind of man he was! He thought of the safety of his friends and bled to death, as we rode several miles that we might be safe. Now he is in the hands of one who fully understands the way Roy died. Jesus Christ, God's son, bled and died that we all might be saved through him. Jesus died that we all might live."

"Father," I prayed, "into thy hands we commit the spirit of Roy Jenkins."

There was a chorus of amens.

We all went to our bed rolls, and I took my Winchester to be a part of the first watch. I was very troubled, and couldn't sleep anyway. Apparently, the last encounter with the scouts had discouraged the Indians. The Pawnee had turned north toward their own village.

I sat and watched the last rays of the sun disappear in the west. My mind was on Roy and the brave way he'd died, and the look of good-bye that came into his eyes as he knew he was dying. My thought went back to that youth who wore the blue uniform in my first battle at Bull Run. His face haunted me; he was surprised, and yet there was a look of terror. His wide-open mouth, ringed with black power from loading his gun, added horror to my own soul. I don't know his name, but I'll never forget the look on his face.

My mind shifted to my own men, and I wondered how Roy's dying would affect them. I knew that they were very adversely affected, for everyone liked Roy. Where was Roy from? Matt had sent him to me and, just maybe, Matt knew his family. I'll not forget him, nor will his friends, for I'll have a head marker made at the fort; and when we turn toward home we will mark his grave.

A night bird called and my mind became that of a sentry as I heard the Whippoorwill begin his series of calls. My mind went to my beloved at the ranch, and I wondered of Delight's safety with Juan Garcia loose. I thought of her gentle ways and her compassion, and then of her fear as she watched the hills as we rode for the ranch after the attack by Garcia. I hoped she was safe, and I wished I was there. That attack by Garcia had discouraged me from sending her to Big Spring and I thought she would be safer at the hacienda. Rex will watch her! Again, the call of the Whippoorwill was much nearer and I became a watchful picket again.

We had no more problems and rode into the fort escorted by an army detail. The fort lay a thousand, fifty-feet east and west, and six hundred feet north and south. It had twenty-two buildings composed of various types of structures and utility. There was an adobe wall enclosing the buildings, and a defensive ditch was dug around the wall. Several cannon were well placed for its defense. Outside the wall and ditch, there were approximately a hundred wigwams. Campfires were strung out among the wigwams and Indian children played games, much to the excitement of barking dogs. The smoke from their campfires hung in the air. Several envious braves watched us, as we drove the horse herd through the gate, and into the fort.

Colonel Canby led us into his office where we reported our

fight with the Indian tribe led by the medicine man. We told of the loss of Roy Jenkins and tried to explain where we'd buried him.

"Your horses all appear to be in good condition," reported the colonel. "They aren't branded, but I'd like to have a bill of sale from you, Mr. McDowell. I believe we've an order with you for a thousand head of cattle. Do you have more cattle available? As you saw when you came in, we've a few guests that must be fed. They're mostly Kiowa and Comanche. We feed them, as there are very few bison these days in this area. We built this fort to help control the Indians in this area; I've found that if we keep some food for them, we can keep them happy. One thousand head of beef is a lot of beef, but know that we can't get it overnight. We've about one hundred head left, and it's very poor quality. When can I expect to get your thousand head of beef?" the colonel asked.

"Colonel, I believe it'll take two weeks to get home and it depends how many can be rounded up and ready for the return trip. There're plenty of cattle, but it takes time to round them up sometimes. I'd say that we should have them back in ten weeks. I'll telegraph you when I'm ready to start the drive," I stated.

"You'll be a sitting duck to old Wolf Head as you come west. I'll try to have you scouted so I can come to meet you and give you some escort. Maybe between the two of us, we can jerk a knot in that old Indian's tail," said the Colonel smiling.

I signed and delivered to the colonel a bill of sale for the horses. He paid me one hundred dollars each for seventy-five of the horses and one hundred twenty-five for twenty-five of the better horses.

I had $10,635 in greenbacks in bundles in my saddlebags. The colonel was interested in Ebony, but understood it was my personal horse and not for sale.

The army blacksmith made an iron cross with Roy Jenkins's name on it and the inscription, "Killed by Indians, August 12, 1866." I paid him ten dollars and put the inscription on a pack horse to carry back to the gravesite with us. The army cook replenished our supplies that the lieutenant had gotten from us when his troop was stranded by the storm.

Early the next morning, we left the fort and headed northeast. Two days later, we found Roy's grave and drove the metal head marker into the ground. We camped there and became very wary as we looked for Indians.

It was the fourth day out that a smoke signal was seen from a ridge about a half mile from us. It was apparent that the Indians had spotted us and were planning to make our return home difficult. Riding and not pushing the herd of horses made our return more mobile, and for three more days we saw nothing of the Indians. In our fourth day, we saw their dust, and it was evident that the whole tribe had come out against us. I told each of our boys to aim to kill. We camped that night on the Pecos River, where Paul said he'd camped on his way back the first time. We were all tired as we sent out pickets, ate our supper, and were soon sound asleep. Just because of the dust I'd seen, I put an extra guard on our horses.

It was early dawn when I heard Ebony whistle, snort, and stamp his foot. I drew my Colt and ran toward where we'd hobbled the horses. Cowboys were rolling out of their blankets, and Winchesters were being cocked. A rifle shot came from down the river and shots were fired near our horses. Several cowboys were putting on their pants with eyes fixed on the horse area. Amos and his scouts were seen running through the woods. Gunfire became continuous, and there were war whoops amidst the sound of the crackle of Winchester repeaters and six-guns.

A thin line of gun smoke hung atop the damp river air and filtered down to hang low over the ground. To my right, I saw two in hand-to-hand combat, and saw my guard holding off an Indian with the butt of his rifle. Amos ran to the guard's assistance and, with his bowie knife, killed the Indian, and then fell on the fallen Indian and scalped him. I remembered Amos had been among Indians so much that he'd taken some of their ways.

Seven or eight Indians were riding toward me screaming and whooping. They were in war paint and were here to kill and take revenge. I shot as fast as I could into their ranks, but two of them were on me before I could turn my gun on them. I had taught hand-to-hand fighting in my company, and fought hard with fury. I swung my rifle butt into the face of an oncoming brave and heard his neck crack; then I swung the gun barrel into the bridge of the nose of a second warrior. Both fell flat and I felt a sharp pain on my left forearm as a warrior slashed at me with his knife. Two shapes formed out of the early morning light next to me, and Amos and Paul were there. Both added their firepower and shot point bank into the charging Indians; and then it was over.

I washed my wound in the nearby river and found it was a slash that had mostly scraped my flesh rather than penetrated. It still hurt, but it could have been worse. I bound it up with some shredded cloth. I wondered why, when the Indians were so near and their numbers were superior, they'd abandoned the battle and left.

We had saved our riding horses and Ebony seemed pleased to see me.

"Anyone see Wolf Head?" I asked

I saw a couple cowboys smile, and when I turned, I drew my Colt with lightening speed and almost shot, when I recognized the cook under the cap of the wolf head. That was the reason the tribe had fled; they'd lost their big medicine man.

"I got him," smiled the cook proudly. He showed off the wolf's head that the chief had worn. He was about to mount his horse, when he pulled the trophy from his head. His smile vanished.

He grabbed a bar of lye soap from the pack horse and, with a snort, rushed for the river. His head was alive with lice and fleas. Laughter shook the men who just a few minutes prior to that time had been fighting for their lives.

The mood changed as they watched the cook scrubbing his bald head, neck, and shoulders with the lye soap. He still held to the wolf head, for it would be his trophy for years to come. His head, face, neck, and shoulders were red for several days from the burning of the soap.

My arm was sore for three days, but I took care of it and favored it when riding. Ebony had given us the proper warning, and we were in high spirits. I don't think we'll need to worry about Wolf Head's tribe for a while.

"They were Pawnee," Paul said. "They are also known as the wolf people; when they are on the war path, they disguise themselves by wearing wolf skins. They sneak up on their enemies, and will shoot them in the back, and it's not their form to confront their enemy or to take needless risks, just as they dealt with us today. They've no friends among other tribes, and old Wolf Head tried to throw us off by speaking Algonquian to me. The tribe will now consult for a new leader. They come from around the Platt River and especially north of the Kiowa. The closest relative to them is the Wichita and that tribe hates them bitterly.

Boss, we'd better watch out for them for a few nights, as they will put on their wolf clothes and try to sneak into our camp and kill us in our sleep," Paul said.

ATTACK ON THE HACIENDA

Tom, (Rex wrote)

I take pen in hand to report the events of this day. This report will cover the activities of my crew until the day of your return. I and the rest of the cowboys that were left behind at the ranch, were very busy branding every head of beef we could find. We coated the raw, burnt hide with grease after the branding to keep the flies off and promote healing. I knew that Juan Garcia was somewhere in the area, so I kept a scout north of the ranch and one south. Delight stayed close to the hacienda and worked in the flower gardens just back of the building. She had an excellent relationship with Erma and worked with her at various projects just to keep busy and to pass the time.

One morning, when we had just completed building our branding fires, a scout came riding in at full gallop from the north.

"Indians!" He cried, and continued on toward the bunkhouse.

We all piled atop of our horses and rode toward the hacienda. Out of the tall grass arose several Indians. Two of the wranglers were killed as they galloped by the savages. The remaining cowboys drew their revolvers and fired point blank into the attackers. One Apache threw a tomahawk, which struck Jess in the back of the head, and he fell to the ground. The savage drew his knife and scalped him.

The gunfire warned the four cowboys at the ranch, and they rushed out to give us covering fire. We abandoned our horses, but took saddle bags and Winchesters into the bunkhouse and the hacienda. Three of the us, including me , rushed for the house, while the other three stayed in the bunkhouse to create crossfire, and cover one another. The storm windows were shut, and the gun portholes were opened. About thirty Apache rode around the two buildings and then vanished from sight.

Erma had her shotgun loaded with buck shot, and Delight went into her bedroom and took two of the Winchesters from the rack and broke open a couple boxes of cartridges. I was by her side to show her how to load the guns.

"You load and I'll shoot," I told her.

I gave covering fire to the bunkhouse. I found your old colt gun and showed Delight how to load it also.

Both buildings had fresh water that had been brought in from the well that morning in case we were surrounded and needed water. There was a case of shells in each building, but the difficulty was that with the storm windows shut, both buildings would become ovens as the sun rose and blazed down. The adobe building stayed cool in the summer with cross ventilation and the windows opened, but it became an oven without the ventilation.

One of the cowboys in the bunkhouse signaled me that there were some Apache at the rear of the hacienda. I opened a port hole and, using my colt revolver, drove the Indians away. When the Indians saw my angle of fire, they leaned against the backside of the house where I couldn't see them. For the rest of the day, we fought off the apaches. I saw Juan Garcia, but couldn't get a shot at him. The Apaches had some older, single-shot guns and were fair shots, so we were cautious when around the port holes.

I missed our southern guard; hoped he had ridden for help and my hope became reality when I heard distance shooting and knew that help was near. The southern guard had heard the firing at the hacienda and had slipped back to see what was amiss. Upon seeing the firing and the Apache in concealed areas, he decided to ride the five hours to town for help from the ranger. Matt gathered forty of the townsmen and rode for the ranch.

About a mile from the ranch, the posse rode into an ambush. Most of the posse were veterans of the war and killed five Apache, while losing as many themselves. I could hear the fighting to the south, and my attention was taken away from the rear of the house to watch the front and give covering fire to whoever was fighting to the south. Two Apache ran their arms through the porthole and unlatched the frame storm window in the back bedroom. The two entered quietly in their moccasin feet. Delight had her back turned to them and was busy loading a Winchester. Delight turned and saw the two walking toward her and she screamed. Erma came out of the kitchen with her shotgun and pulled both triggers, and fired buckshot into the breast of one of the Apache. The other lifted his bow and shot an arrow into Delight.

I came from the parlor and shot from the hip with my Winchester at the remaining Indian, who was about to scalp Delight. Erma looked down at Delight's sightless eyes, dropped her shotgun, and screamed. Outside, there came the sound of pounding hoofs and the sound of gunfire as the posse rushed upon the porch. The rescue from town had arrived. This ends my report for it was but a few minutes that you all arrived. Boss, this is the worst day of my life. I have great sorrow about the outcome.

The report was signed by Rex.

THE WELCOME HOME

Amos and Paul confronted me as we crossed the river.

"Tom, we've come across a large number of unshod horse tracks. They don't appear to be a day old, but they're headed toward the ranch, or in that direction," said Paul.

This caused me great concern, and it was apparent that Amos and Paul felt the same.

"Let's hurry along," I said.

"Rex is there, and those guys won't let anything happen to her," said Paul.

It was a good five-hour ride to the ranch, and I turned Ebony toward home. Amos and Paul rode by my side with the rest of the group coming along behind. The black stallion could easily outrun the other horses, so I gave him his head and he glided in a swift, smooth motion.

"Let's go help her, Ebony, old boy!" I whispered in his ear.

Paul wasn't far behind as we approached the ranch, and both horses were winded and blowing. I was scared as I heard gunfire and saw Indians on horses circling the hacienda and bunkhouse. Four Indians came from behind the blacksmith shop to cut us off. I shot into the group, not aiming, and missed. My terror had caused me to not aim, so I'd failed to be accurate. I corrected my gun and shot two of the approaching Indians, and the remaining two lifted their bows and shot past me. I heard Paul grunt and knew he'd been hit, for he fell sideways from his horse. I stopped and fired at the two Indians, and managed to hit them both.

I saw Juan Garcia riding past the bunkhouse, but before I could shoot, he was gone. Men were streaming out of the hacienda, and

I recognized men from town. *The ranger must be here,* I thought. Two men cheered me from the bunkhouse as the rest of my cowboys came bounding up behind me. I turned and rode back to Paul. Amos was kneeling by his side, holding his head.

"Is it bad?" I asked, and he nodded yes.

I leaped from Ebony and sat down in the dirt by my ramrod. One look at his face, and I knew Paul was dead!

"Oh, no!" I cried. "He took that arrow for me. He could've held back or faded to left or right, but he put his horse into the line of fire and they focused on him rather than me."

"Tom," said a familiar voice, "easy boy!"

It was the livery man from town.

"Matt's in the house, but maybe you'd better not go in."

What he said caused me to leap to my feet and I almost fell as I turned toward him.

"Was Matt hit?" I asked.

"No sir, but—"

His look shook me.

"No, no!" I cried, as I turned and rushed toward the hacienda.

I bounded onto the porch and looked through the parlor and living room toward the back bedrooms. Matt was sitting on the floor with Delight's head on his shoulder, swaying back and forth and sobbing. Her head tilted toward me and I looked into her beautiful face. The green sightless eyes were just as beautiful as they'd always been, but they were blank and didn't focus on me. Her golden hair was hanging in ringlets down her back and was damp from perspiration. Her dimple and her usual smile were gone; she looked to be asleep and so innocent.

"Oh, my Delight! Tom, they've killed our Delight," called Matt.

Tears flowed down my cheeks as I sat down by them and put my arms about them both. I took my handkerchief and tried to wipe a spot of dried blood from her cheek.

The Indian who'd killed her lay three feet away with a knife in one hand and some long strands of blond hair in his other hand. Someone had shot him just as he was about to scalp her. The

Apache arrow that had pierced her chest had gone all the way through her body; she'd died instantly.

I sat with my head between my knees as my cowboys came in with hats in hand and tears in their eyes. Rex was taking it hard, and he explained the situation to his friends. They knew it wasn't his fault. I was taking the blame for not taking her to her mother to stay while I was gone.

Erma came and closed Delight's eyes and, with a cloth, washed and cleaned the blood from her face. Erma had her taken to our bed, and she was washed and clothed in her very best clothing. Matt and I planned for a family grave site on a slight hill amidst the flower gardens that she loved so well. Our blacksmith made a wrought iron fence to surround the cemetery. The families of the cowboys who'd been killed were all notified and agreed to have them buried as a part of our TM Ranch family. I had a stone made for the both of us and then saved a place by her side for me and two on her other side for Matt and Bess. A grave was dug for Paul and five very faithful cowboys who had died defending the TM Ranch.

I read and reread Rex's report to me. Rex had done the right thing in turning his attention to the Posse to give them support. I thought of Paul, how he might be alive if I had taken more time in aiming at the approaching Indians. The entire day was a tragedy that would plague me the rest of my life. I put no blame on Rex.

The funeral was very well attended, for nearly the whole town turned out to see my Delight for the last time. I had stones made for Paul and the five cowboys alike, and on Paul's tombstone I had etched the words, "He died in my stead."

The minister from town came out and presided over the funeral and all seven were buried at the same time. I spoke a few words about Paul and the cowboys. "Greater love hath no man than this that he lay down his life for his friends." It was Goldie Williams who had taught me that scripture. Those cowboys had been true to the brand. They'd died trying to protect those who made up the TM Ranch. Paul had died for me and it pained me so to know what he'd done. His beard had been trimmed and he looked handsome lying there in a black broadcloth suit. I clothed all five cowboys like I had clothed Paul.

Melody came and sat with Matt and Bess, and the three held one another as they shared the agony of their loss. Melody, Matt, and Bess stayed the night at the hacienda and Matt took them both back to town in the surrey.

I gave the men a couple days off and some men went to town, while others went into the fields and worked and grieved over their lost friends. I had to get away, for everything I saw reminded me of Delight. She really loved the ranch and the vast blue of the Texas sky. The flowers were blooming still and the dwellings showed no wear from the ordeal of the Apache attack. I needed to get away from the ranch, so I told Rex to continue branding cattle and gathering them so we could make a cattle drive when I got back.

THE SOLACE OF THE HIGH COUNTRY

The great high plains lie to the west of my ranch and are at the foot of the Rocky Mountains. Separating the high plains from the lower plains is a rocky ridge called Cap Rock. The Cap Rock rises approximately one thousand feet, and it was along this that I rode Ebony. I longed to be healed from all the sorrow and death that I'd experienced in the past week.

I found a small missionary church and spent an uplifting day as the preacher talked to me of the healing presence of Jesus Christ. I sat alone in the front pew of the little church building and called upon my God and poured out my troubles to him. I'd done this before in a small, brick church house called Salem Church, west of Fredericksburg. I'd knelt and found relief from the ordeals of battle. The front of that building was a hospital operating room where the arms and legs of the amputees had been piled six feet deep. I'd seen so many die in various ways, and it'd been a time when I needed to fly to God for refuge. The face of that first boy that I killed at Bull Run, continued to plague me. Both North and South had found Salem Church house to be a place of help.

For two weeks, I rode and prayed and thought of Delight. Sweet Bess, in a tender moment as we remembered Delight, said for my benefit, "Tom, I'm sure that you know that she knew Jesus Christ as her personal Savior. Let's see, it has been eleven years ago that she met her Lord and was baptized into Christ and was born again. She told me how she loved to pray with you since her marriage and, though this terrible tragedy makes Matt and me so sad, she is with her Lord now."

It was this bit of knowledge that gave me joy in the middle of my sadness, and I came to myself and knew that my cowboys were waiting for me at home. I turned Ebony to the north and rode slowly back to the ranch.

THE CATTLE DRIVE

I decided not to sleep at the hacienda, but to use one of the bunks in the bunkhouse. The cowboys realized that I couldn't go back to my bed right then and went out of their way not to say anything that might remind me of Delight. I promoted Rex to foreman and instructed him to continue branding beef until we reached at least a thousand one hundred. We'd have an extra hundred head to trade or work with on the trail. We searched through the fields and got as many cattle as we could gather. The branding was extra hard work, for we were working now with older cattle. We left cows in the fields that had dropped calves recently, but made sure the cows were branded.

One evening, Rex came in and told me that we'd met our quota, but wouldn't be sure until we could get a more accurate count. I told him to keep them in holding pens until I could get to town to telegraph the fort that we were on the way.

I saddled Ebony and rode for town the next morning. It was the middle of September 1866, and the leaves were at their peak in color. There was a slight chill in the air and the goldenrod and other wildflowers added to the beauty of the countryside. "This is the day that the Lord has made I will rejoice and be glad in it." The verse came to my mind from scriptures learned from Goldie Williams, the kind, black mother of my childhood. Ebony wanted to lope along, and I gave him the reins. I had him broken to the bridle, and not neck broken as most cowboys wanted their horses.

•

I found the town just as it'd been the last time I was there, but sadness built in my mind as I neared the jail, and the ranger's post. Matt stood staring at me, and I knew that seeing me brought to his mind the blond girl that both of us loved

"Hi, Son," he called.

"God bless you, Dad," I replied.

I sat there on Ebony for a moment and smiled at him. I believe he'd lost weight, and the lines on his face showed the results of extreme sorrow.

"Get down and come in, or would you like to go to the restaurant for a cup of coffee?" he asked.

"I'll buy," I offered.

It was nearly ten thirty, so there were few in the restaurant. Melody was there, and she came with her pad. The girl was not at fault, but she reminded me first of Delight and then of Paul.

"Hello, Tom. Hello, Matt," she said.

"Hi, Melody. Could we get a cup of coffee and a piece of pie?" I asked.

"Got some dried apple pie left," she said.

"Sounds good," I answered. "How have you been?"

"Getting by, but times are hard," she replied, and she was off for the pie and coffee. I turned back to Matt.

"How's Bess?" I asked.

"I'm worried about her, Tom. She's just pined away. She keeps losing weight and very seldom smiles. We both know what's bothering her," answered Matt.

"Boy, do I know how she feels. I haven't moved back into the hacienda since, you know, since it happened. I'm trying to immerse myself in my work, and I know my melancholy has rubbed off on Rex and the crew," I added.

"Women mourn deeper than us men, I guess. I've been hoping that Bess would get straightened up, Tom, but I just don't know. We both loved Delight so very much, and I know you did too," said Matt.

"Matt, I need to send a telegram to the fort that I have my cattle ready and plan to try to deliver them as soon as we can get the roundup done. I plan to have them at the fort by around the middle of November, weather permitting." I said.

Melody was back with the pie and two cups of coffee. Her blue eyes were centered on me.

"Tom, you've lost a little weight. Are you taking care of yourself? Been eating well?" she questioned me.

"Melody, I'm all right, but as you said, it's hard," I replied.

"We're having a different type of customers coming in here. They're carpetbaggers from the North, and they're hard to please. They're insulting and very domineering and make it difficult for me. Here come some now," she said.

Four men had entered the restaurant, and it was apparent that they were from the North, for they looked harshly toward the ranger.

"You've been having trouble with these guys, Matt?" I asked in a whisper.

"Yes. I knew that it was coming and it has taken a year in getting here, but believe me, it's here now" answered Matt. "These four men that just came in are an example of a lot of the riff-raff that's plaguing our state. They about all have chips on their shoulders and make our women live hard. They've come down here to try to influence and promote some ex-slave to hold public office. Here comes one now," said Matt.

"Hello, Ranger! I want to make a complaint about one of your rangers. He doesn't seem to realize that my partners and I here are now paying your wages. I've found some abandoned land and I'm living there now. I and my friends aim to buy the place according to the Freedmen's Act. I think you know that Mr. Lorrie had to leave here when he refused to leave the Union. His lands were abandoned, and we're here to take them back in his name. Your deputy ranger hasn't seen it the way we'uns does and pulled a gun on us out at our own place."

"The thing that you speak of isn't exactly as my deputy said that it happened. I believe you'll need to drop by my office and make out a complaint," Matt said.

"Listen to me, Ranger! You ain't going to sweep this thing under the rug. I know my rights. You git back to your office and put him under arrest. We'll sign a complaint then."

"Stop it!" screamed Melody and pulled her arm away from one of the men who was trying to get her on his lap.

He grabbed her again and she slapped him. He got ugly then and rose up from the table to strike her. I stood up and, in so doing, my chair fell over backwards.

"Oh, you want in this, do you?" asked the tormentor, looking at me.

"You're a little drunk, and you can see the lady doesn't want you to paw her," I said.

He grinned and swung at me as hard as he could. It was a round-house swing, which I easily avoided. His miss caused him to fall heavily. Another of the four was now on his feet and came to help his friend. My punch only traveled about a yard and caught him as he was coming in, and right on the chin. His body hit the floor hard, and he slid to the wall with a crash. The first man was getting up, so I kneed him. I put my hands behind his head and pulled his head down while I lifted my knee. He laid stretched out on the floor and turned red, and then purple, as he gasped for breath. I caught movement at the table, for the remaining man was reaching for his gun. My Colt 44 suddenly appeared in my hand where there had been no gun, and he froze and stared at me. Slim's training me in the fast draw had paid off. I looked down at my weapon and saw that it was cocked and ready to fire. I'd trained for months on my draw and was almost as much amazed as they were. The gunman hadn't cleared his holster, and he stared at me in terror.

"I don't want any of you men bothering Melody here. Do you understand me? When you drew your gun down here in Texas, I could've killed you, for it'd have been self-defense; that's the way we live down here. You came this close to seeing what hell is like," I said, and held up my left hand and measured an inch with my thumb and finger.

I turned to the tormenter who was coming to and sitting up on the floor.

"You keep your hands to yourself, and I don't want anyone

bothering Melody or you'll hear from me. You understand? Now, you tell her you are sorry and won't do it again!"

I pointed my gun at the blanching man.

"I'm sorry, miss!" he said, and his eyes didn't leave my cocked gun.

"Now git!" I said, and the four ran out of the restaurant.

Matt turned to me and grinned.

"Thanks, Tom! I believe you have cured those four, for you put fear in them. You see why I wanted you as a deputy, for there is something steely in you that shows no fear; men will back off from that look in you," said Matt.

"I didn't know that I could draw my gun like that. I've been practicing but never had to use it till now. Slim Wilkins did a good job teaching me that fast draw," I said.

"Thanks, Tom," said Melody.

"Melody, you don't have to put up with being pawed like that. You tell me if it happens again, and I'll throw them in jail," said Matt.

We finished our coffee and pie and went on to the telegraph office, where my message was sent to the fort. The cook left the restaurant just after Matt and I and headed to the saloon. Soon, the entire town was abuzz as the episode was repeated again and again.

I stopped by to see Bess as I was leaving town. She was glad to see me, and I hugged and kissed her. I called her Mom, which made her smile.

"Oh, get on with you!"

I promised her that after we got back from delivering the cattle, I'd drop by for a few days. She smiled, and I saw right then that one thing she needed was love and affection. She wanted to mother someone. I hugged and kissed her once again; then I gathered up the reins and mounted Ebony.

I looked back down the street, and there was Melody, watching and waving good-bye. I felt guilty because Delight had been dead just a little while, but I rode down the street to where Melody was standing.

"Melody, Bess needs someone to mother and I think it'd be

beneficial to both of you if you told her you loved her and needed her love in return. Matt also needs someone to look after. You all are so dear to me. Trust God and he will sustain all of you. Good-bye, Melody!"

"Good-bye, and thanks, Tom," she whispered.

•

I clucked to Ebony and swung him around toward home. Again, I rode the trail back toward the ranch and watched the hills, especially when I came to the place where we'd been ambushed.

My trip back to the ranch was uneventful, and when I arrived home, there was smoke in the air; the cowboys had been branding. Hundreds of cattle were in the corrals, and the TM was plain on their hips.

"I've hired five additional cowboys from men sent out from town that Matt recommended," said Rex, and he called them and introduced them to me.

After they went back to work, Rex continued.

"Those five have been to work since you've been gone, and they're fitting in among the crew well. I believe we've enough personnel to make this drive and still have a crew here to watch the place while we're gone."

I rode to the bunkhouse and, amid a chorus of "Howdy," began to return their greetings, and then gathered my things. They pretended not to notice that I was moving back into the hacienda. When I opened the door to the hacienda, there was an overjoyed Erma and a smiling cook.

"Welcome home," they cried.

"I've changed your bed linen, and the entire house has been cleaned and plaster has been repaired and repainted where it were damaged from gunfire," said Erma.

It was as she'd said, and the dark stains had been scraped from the floor, and the floor had been refinished. It was as if the whole thing was a terrible nightmare. I carried my clothes into the master bedroom and the poster bed had been moved slightly. The windows let in a flood of light, and I sat there and came to a decision that my mourning was over and I couldn't bring her back.

I had dinner with the cowboys and went to work with a vengeance. We'd a lot of work to do, and I was determined to meet our time requirements and get the herd there on time. I had on the deerskin jacket that old chief Wolf Fang had given me as a gift. It would be the middle of November when we delivered the herd to the fort. I called Amos and asked him how far our trail would miss Wolf Fang's campsite.

"We'll be approximately two hours ride from it," answered Amos.

"Good. When we drive the herd that close to his camp, I want you to take twenty-five head of cattle and drive them over to him as my gift. Then, on the way back, we'll all stop and enjoy a Thanksgiving meal with his tribe. While we're there, I want to hunt with him and smoke the peace pipe."

Amos smiled.

"He'll really enjoy that! I know he's my father-in-law, but he's an excellent chief and a good Indian," he said.

"I've gifts for him and his son, which I feel they'll enjoy other than the cattle. I've two shotguns and a case of ten and twelve gauge shells and different sized shot, which I'll take for the shotguns," I said.

Amos smiled broadly.

"Boss, don't forget that rum tobacco; Wolf Fang would like to know how to grow tobacco with that kind of flavor. I'd like that secret too."

"I've still got a few tins left, but I need to order some more just in case I'll need it. Think I'll order some cigars too," I added.

I called my cowboys to the hacienda for supper, and we all gathered around the big table while Erma and the cook served us. Following an excellent meal, I permitted them to smoke and jaw for a little while. I stood at the front of the table and banged my spoon on my glass. They all turned their attention to me.

"I understand that we've about 1,250 head of cattle ready for our trip to the fort. I want ten of you to stay here and twelve to drive the herd. Rex will select who'll go and who'll stay. Rex will be in charge as ramrod on the road. Amos will be in charge of the scouts, and that leaves George Cavenaugh to be in charge of those here at the ranch. George, this will be new to you, but I've confidence that you can do a good job. It may well be that the Apache will be watching us leave and thus be planning to hit us again. I'm going to contact the ranger station for some help. Erma, I want you to take the surrey and go to town and stay while we're gone. I'll send money with you so that you can stay at the hotel until we get back. Also, I'll send a note with you for Matt. Any questions?" I asked.

George Cavenaugh was one of the cowboys who was exceptionally good with a six-gun and had given me a few pointers on a fast draw. He'd been an officer in the army and was very able to command in my absence. He was of medium built, had dark hair and eyes, a mustache, sideburns, and a partial beard.

"Cook, we plan to have a Thanksgiving meal with the Kiowa, so take plenty of provisions for an excellent dinner," I instructed. "We'll leave at dawn, and Erma, I want you to be ready to leave at that time too," I stated. "Good night!"

They all moved out of the dining room and began to make final preparations.

•

It was still dark when I awakened to the smell of coffee and bacon. Several of the cowboys were at the table, and all were wide awake and eager to get started. They were joking, and there was some horse play. They loved to kid Erma and the cook as if he had something going with Erma. Actually, several of the older cowboys were interested in Erma and wanted to assist her on her trip into town. After all, she needed someone to go along and drive the surrey and see to it that she'd a place to stay at the hotel. George Cavenaugh appointed one of the oldest cowboys to go and several appeared disappointed.

"I think George likes Erma, himself," I said under my breath.

The chuck wagon was filled with food, and there were three pack horses also laden with supplies. One pack horse held my ten gauge shotgun and two cases of shells, including various shot sizes.

I also had my twelve -gauge shotgun with shells. All the cowboys sat their horses, and I took off my hat and prayed for a peaceful trip and the safety of my men. We replaced our hats, and I turned to Rex and said, "Rex, let's go!"

"Ya ha!" he screamed.

The call was answered by the Confederate rebel cry as men waved their hats to get the cattle up and moving.

"Amos, Rex, lead us out of here!" I cried.

The old mossy bulls were up front and the Texas longhorns were all moving. Rex had the cowboys rotate so that not every person would have to eat and breathe the dust of the vast herd. Erma, with her escort, flashed down the trail toward town and waved a fond good-bye to her men. Every cowboy lifted his hat in response and cheered, and she was gone. The red and brown surrey flashed in the morning sun.

We'd like to average fifteen miles a day, but wanted good, fat cattle to be delivered and wanted them watered whenever possible. The weather was good, but the land was dry. Our cloud of dust could be seen for many miles. This drive was new to the area, as there hadn't been a market for that many cattle in years. We crossed the Sulphur Draw and headed west toward New Mexico.

I figured it'd take us a month to get to the fort, if we had no problems. Various times we saw Indian hunting parties, and a time or two we cut out a few steers as a gift to them. We were thankful that we'd few problems with them. Amos and two cowboys cut out one hundred fifty head of cattle from the herd and drove them to his father-in-law's Kiowa camp. This was about four days before we reached the fort. Two days out of Fort Craig, we were met by an escort of Yankee cavalry.

Colonel Canopy had been replaced, but the new officer had my telegram and was very gracious in his welcome. He claimed those at the fort could see our dust for miles. Every Indian tribe would have scouts out to see what was causing the dust. Could the bison be back? Indians flocked to the fort and the commanding officer permitted many to have cattle. We were busy counting the number of cattle that were slaughtered just outside the fort. The Indians were hungry and most eager for the beef.

"You saved the day!" cried Colonel George Herring.

He introduced himself and his staff to us. I recognized the burley old first sergeant and nodded to him. We spent three or four days resting up, and then I called our group together and we started back. I had six thousand dollars in greenbacks in my saddlebags. Horses were much more valuable, but what I got for the cattle cheered me. The colonel indicated that he'd telegraph me with additional orders for both horses and beef.

BEEF FOR THE KIOWA

We made about forty miles a day, and then one morning at the end of the week we saw Indians. There must have been a hundred braves led by Wolf Fang and Amos, and they were there to escort us into their village. They came with hands lifted high, and old Wolf Fang was smiling and calling: "Welcome!" He spoke to me in the Kiowa language, and Amos interpreted.

"He thanks you for all that beef. They've been eating their favorite parts, the tongues and the livers."

"I like other parts better," I said, knowing the Kiowa didn't understand my thoughts or my language.

There must have been at least 150 wigwams that comprised the village, and not only were there cattle, but the village had a nice-sized horse herd. Amos was my spokesman and interpreted the words of Wolf Fang. From Rex I knew that the Kiowa came from Arkansas and the Platte river area and they called themselves a Kayowe man and were either a part of the Comanche or a close relative. They were fierce people and brave fighters. Wolf Fang was a great chief, clean, and had the respect of his people. His smile and behavior caused me to like him. I was directed to the chief's tent and was pleasantly surprised when I entered. The dirt floor was covered with rugs made from the skins of various animals, and the sun illuminated the tepee. There was a fire in the middle of the wigwam, and an open area directly above so the tent was ventilated. Wolf Fang introduced his two wives. One of his wives kept looking at my jacket.

"This is Little Doe. She's the number one wife and the mother of my wife," interpreted Amos. "I added that about my wife," he grinned. "This is White Song." He pointed to the second woman, who was much younger.

"Tell them I am pleased to meet Wolf Fang and his two wives," I said. "Tell the cook to bring up my pack animals with the gifts."

Little Doe pointed to my deer jacket and smiled. I nodded to her that I knew she had made the jackets. The cook came through the door with several aluminum pots and iron skillets. He also had a butcher knife and a meat cleaver. Both Little Doe and White Song seemed enchanted with them. I spread the gifts between them. They smiled and chattered to each other.

"Bring me that ten-gauge shotgun," I said.

It was a double-barreled, heavy gun. I'd brought several boxes of shells of various size shot.

"Tell the chief that it shoots hard and different sized shot should be used on different animals when he hunts," I told Amos. "Would you like to see it shoot?" I asked, speaking to the chief.

The chief took the gun in his hand and looked it over. I showed him how to break it open and how to load it. I showed him the safety and how to pull back the hammers as well as which trigger fired which barrel. He was fascinated and called for his son to come with us.

We walked outside and I led the way to the edge of the village. Every warrior, squaw, and child, as well as all the dogs followed along behind. Amos was talking, explaining to all what I aimed to do. At the edge of the clearing, I stopped and pointed out a dead tree that was about to fall from decay. I loaded both barrels and demonstrated how to hold the gun and how to aim and turn off the safety. The top trigger shot the left barrel, I explained, and the second trigger shot the right barrel. I aimed and the powerful gun boomed. The limb was torn from the tree and pieces of bark and dust flew in all directions. The blast roared through the entire village and several uttered excitedly in the Kiowa language.

I broke open the gun and pulled out the smoking shotgun shell, which was a light load. I looked at the other side, and it had a heavy load. I offered the gun to the chief and he motioned to his son to shoot the gun first. The brave walked forward and took the gun from me. I showed him which trigger to pull and showed him how to look along the top of the gun and point the bead at the target. He nodded and held the gun about an inch off his shoulder and pulled till his face turned red, but the gun did not shoot. I showed him that the safety had to be off. I was about to tell him how to hold the gun when he switched off the safety took aim and pulled the trigger. The limb shattered in a puff of sawdust. The gun kicked back in a very savage manner and struck the brave, and he hit the dirt on his back.

The whole village stepped back as the brave got up. He dusted himself off and uttered several choice words in the Kiowa language.

Amos said, "Ugh! Big kick!"

Everyone laughed. He was a rider and was familiar with the kick of a horse. He'd made the comparison, not realizing that he used the same term that the white man did in describing the kick of a shotgun. Of course, he spoke in Kiowa and I didn't understand what he'd said. Amos interpreted, and I laughed with the village. I had Amos explain about holding the gun tight against the shoulder and to give with the kick. I also told Amos to tell about the different size loads of powder in the shells. The brave smiled as he held the gun, and new shells were placed in the gun. This time, he waited till I showed him how to hold the gun and how to rebound with the kick. He aimed and shot a third limb from the tree. He rebounded with the kick, and he smiled at the chief with satisfaction.

"Tell the chief that I give him this gun and all these shells as a present for being a good friend," I said to Amos, and he interpreted.

THANKSGIVING WITH THE KIOWA

"Many years ago, my white brothers came from far lands in a big ship. They found friendship with their red brothers, and they shared their foods with them in a gesture of thanksgiving to the Great Spirit. You know of the war fought between the people of the North and the people of the South. Abraham Lincoln asked the people of the North to set aside the fourth Thursday of this month as a day to offer thanks. He wanted especially to offer thanks for the winning of a battle, the battle of Gettysburg. I fought in that battle and survived because of God's great grace to me. I'd like to offer a Thanksgiving feast to him this coming Thursday, which is three more suns away. On that third day, will you share with us a feast of gladness and friendship and give thanks to the Great Spirit?"

"It is good! We'll eat together and say thanks to the Great Spirit," said Wolf Fang.

The chief led us all back to the wigwam, where we met a very beautiful young girl. She was wearing a white deerskin dress, and her hair was black and braided into two parts. There were beads sewn into her garments and plaited in her hair. Her eyes were a dark brown, and her lips were full. She was about five feet and six inches tall, had a beautiful figure, and was shy.

"Come little one," said Wolf Fang, and Amos interpreted to me.

"She's his daughter by his second wife, White Song, and half sister to my wife," said Amos. "His son, Red Hand, was the brave that shot the shotgun, and a full brother to my wife."

"What's the girl's name?" I asked.

"Her name is Causes to Laugh," said Amos. "White Song and Wolf Fang had no children for several years. When Causes to Laugh was born, White Song had given up believing she could bear a child. The coming of the beautiful child caused her to laugh."

"She is indeed a delightful, beautiful girl," I said.

A green-eyed beautiful face came into my mind, and I could see Delight's smile and the dimple. My mind went back to Delight and the short happiness that we had together.

I sat with Wolf Fang and his son that afternoon, and, with Amos as interpreter, we went over many things. Red Hand appeared to be a solid-thinking young man and would one day make an excellent chief. We sat at their fire, and I brought out the rum tobacco. The aroma was very pleasing, and the chief enjoyed it greatly. I presented him with a large bag of the tobacco as a gift.

"Ask the chief if there are any turkeys in the woods here," I said to Amos.

The chief nodded yes.

"I'd love to hunt them tomorrow and would like Wolf Fang and Red Hand to hunt with me," I said.

Amos interpreted and the old chief smiled yes, as did Red Hand. I left them and went out where they'd slaughtered one of the longhorns. I took a hand saw used by the cook and sawed off the end of a bull's horn. I walked back and noticed the wondering eyes of Red Hand and Wolf Fang. I cupped the horn in my hands and perfectly mimicked the call of a Tom turkey. Immediately, both Indians were interested, and I showed them how to suck on the horn and to cup their hands. Red Hand tried several times and then Wolf Fang, but neither could fool a live turkey and they knew it. Red Hand went outside and soon came back in with a piece of grass that he laid across his tongue. He mimicked the perfect "*kee, kee*" of a hen turkey. All smiled and I went out to my pack and found some number four shot for the ten-gauge.

"This is the size shot to use in the ten-gauge gun when hunting turkey," I said.

Amos repeated it to them in Kiowa. Both Wolf Fang and Red Hand were interested. I'd brought my twelve-gauge shotgun along to hunt the turkey with Wolf Fang. I went out and got it with a box of shells.

"Red Hand, you use my twelve-gauge gun, and I'll use my Winchester."

It tickled Red Hand as he broke open the gun and looked carefully at it. It was an excellent gun and could be used for quail or turkey. The next morning, we slipped out of the village before daylight, and Red Hand pointed to a distant forest. The Indians walked so silently that I was impressed. I had on my own moccasins, but I made much more noise walking than they.

We all climbed a hill that was covered with mountain laurel, and near the top of the hill were several large oak trees. There we settled down, and I saw large amounts of turkey scratching under the trees. Red Hand was pointing them out to me. I nodded and he sat down, and I went about five hundred feet farther on. I found good cover and sat behind a huge oak with a lot of underbrush about me. Everything was quiet. Suddenly, I heard a turkey fly down from his roost. I heard the "*kee, kee*" of Red Hand's call, and then I gave the answer of the old Tom with my horn.

A blast from the twelve-gauge shattered the quiet of the morning. Off a good half mile, I heard "*boom, boom,*" as Wolf Head shot at a turkey. I couldn't help but grin, for they had both emptied their guns. A large Tom turkey flew into a tree fifty yards from me, and I saw where he landed. I slowly lifted my rifle, and he stirred on the limb and turned around toward me. I slipped my horn into my mouth and putted once. The turkey's head went straight up as he attempted to locate me. I pulled the trigger on my Golden Boy and he fell head first to the ground.

Everything became very quiet again. I could see the turkey lying there, so I didn't move. I lifted my horn and gave the assembly call. I was answered by two different turkeys. I could hear one running toward me, and he came within twenty-five feet as he ran by. I turned and I shot the head off a fine gobbler. I heard a clucking of the third turkey, and when I answered, the hen flew straight up into a tree and I shot her. Hunting in Orange County, Virginia for turkey was good, but this was wonderful. It was all that I could do to carry all three birds back to camp. Wolf Fang and Red Hand both had good gobblers. Wolf Fang and Red Hand were happy, not only for the meat but for the tail and wing feathers which they'd use in their head bonnets.

They were surprised when I showed them my three turkeys. All three of my turkeys had been shot in the head or neck.

We took the turkeys back to the village, and Little Doe and White Song immediately took them and began to clean them. Causes to Laugh came to me and took my three turkeys, smiled, and began dry-plucking them. That night, we sat about the camp fire while the tribe danced their special dance for our successful hunting trip. I had to insist that our cook would be the one who cooked the turkeys that I'd killed. I was looking forward to the dressing and the giblet gravy.

The last Thursday of November came at last, and the cook was up before dawn. The delicious aroma filled the air, and several Indian women stood watching. He planned his meal well and called on a cowboy or two to stir something to keep it from burning. The day moved slowly along, and his labor mounted. His cherry, apple, pumpkin, and squash pies were looked on by the Indian squaws in amazement. He poured milk from a can and made heaps of mashed potatoes. He stirred some of the milk into his gravy. His extra big fireside oven that he brought, especially for this occasion, held one turkey after another until all were done to perfection. He lifted a large pan and banged it with a copper spoon. Now all the cowboys, plus Amos, Rex, and I knew what that sound meant, but the Indians just stood and looked with alarm at the scene before them. Amos ran for Chief Wolf Fang and Red Hand and told them what the banging of the pan meant.

They called and the people came with items of their own cooked meals. There was venison, elk, trout, quail, and turkey. They had greens and parched corn. There was also wild honey and corn cakes. I greeted the whole tribe, and then I spoke to them all, with Amos as the interpreter.

"Hear, Chief Wolf Fang, Red Hand, all of you fine braves, my cowboys, and all friends! We wish to express to our God our thanks and appreciation for all he has done. I thank my God for your friendship and all this plenteous food." I lifted both my arms into the air as Paul the Apostle told his son, Timothy, to do in faith. "I thank you for life, your Son, and your great Spirit."

There was a murmur among the Indians and they all lifted their hands when they heard of the Spirit. A chant began among the Indians that lasted for a few minutes. I dropped my arms and said "Amen." All the cowboys said, "Amen," and we sat down. The cook called for some help and began to pass out the food. The Indian women, not to be outdone, came with their food. Some used fingers, some used sharp knives, some used both hands, but the purpose was the same: they ate! Mouths were bulging with food, and they ate and ate and ate. The pies were cut, and the Indians tasted and smacked their lips. All rejoiced, laughed, and told stories in tongues that only some partially understood. The cowboys slapped the braves on the back and got a good lick in return. I looked at the two happy groups, and I rejoiced. I must tell them more about the Great Spirit that I know. Maybe both groups need to know more. We helped the cook clean his pots and pans, but there were many squaws there to help a white man do women's work. The braves looked at the cook in amazement as he washed the pots and pans.

•

Later that night, a very stern Amos approached me.

"Boss, you've a real problem. Chief Wolf Fang just spoke to me about Causes to Laugh. You've given the Chief all of these gifts, and he has nothing of value that even compares to offer you in return. He wants to give to you his greatest possible gift. He wants to give to you his daughter, Causes to Laugh. She has been approached by her father and is more than willing to be your mate for life.

"Usually, the young Kiowa brings horses to the father, and the girl considers his offer and says yes or no to the offer. Causes to Laugh knows that you gave her dad twenty-five horses and that you're a great hunter and wants you as her husband. Boss, this is very serious stuff, for if you refuse her it'd be an insult to her and to her dad. When I married my wife, I gave Wolf Fang five horses and she said yes. I must admit that I courted her for a good month before she agreed to be my wife," said Amos.

"Causes to Laugh is a delightful girl, but I must admit I'm not in love with her and don't even know her. I still think of Delight. It's still too soon to even consider remarriage. Amos, get me out of this!" I pleaded.

"You've hit the nail on the head! Whenever a Kiowa brave is killed in battle, the Kiowa people mourn his death by the women cutting their hair short. Those close to him give his things away so that he'll not be remembered. Boss, I could tell them that the white mon is different and that when a white mon loses his wife that he loves, he doesn't even think of other womon, but thinks and mourns over his wife day and night for some time until his mourning for her has passed."

"Amos, that is true too. Speak to Wolf Fang and have him convey it on to Causes to Laugh. I need some time to straighten this out," I said. "I'll send the crew on back home, for I don't trust the Apache. Rex can continue to ramrod the ranch. You stay here with me, as I want to help this girl and her dad to understand how I feel and why I can't accept."

"Ah, I'll stay; you'll need all the help that you can get," said Amos.

The next morning, I was up early, but Causes to Laugh wasn't in her bed. Amos was also gone. I had breakfast with my crew, and we talked about the ranch and about getting back to work there.

"Rex, I want you to take the boys and hurry on back to the ranch. Amos and I need to stay here for a while, as I see a problem that needs to be addressed. When you get back to the ranch, send for Erma and bring her back from town. The ranch is her home, and I want her to know that. I want you boys to hunt that whole area around our ranch for cattle. There may be a lot of Don's cattle in those hills and valleys. Find them and brand them if they aren't branded, and run them back to our ranch. If they are branded; then leave them alone, as well as their calves. I want all of our calves branded. I want you to use that box canyon and catch as many wild horses as you can. I'm not sure just how long I'll be here, but I'll have Amos with me."

"Yes, sir," said Rex, but I knew he'd no idea what'd happened to make me want to stay out here and not go home. They mounted up, but left me with some spare ammunition. I also took the twelve-gauge shotgun with all its ammunition. They rode out, anxious to get back home. Red Hand came and I gave him the twelve-gauge shotgun with all my shells, and he was very pleased.

"I want to hunt bison with you if I can," I told Amos to tell them.

They were pleased that I'd stayed. If they knew about my difficulty about Causes to Laugh, they didn't mention it. I didn't see Causes to Laugh until that evening, and there wasn't a smile on her face when she looked at me.

"Tell her that I need to speak with her," I told Amos.

He spoke to her and she looked at me with angry eyes.

She spoke in a loud voice so that all could hear. "Everyone knows my shame. Why you shamed me?"

"Amos, have them all assemble in the wigwam, and let's get this over with," I said.

"They're already assembled there," said Amos.

I walked into the wigwam, and it was true. There sat Wolf Fang, Red Hand, White Song, Little Doe, and Causes to Laugh. Causes to Laugh had tears in her eyes and was remote. I began to speak and gave Amos time to interpret my English into language that they understood.

"Causes to Laugh is not on trial here. Her desire to marry me is one of the greatest graces of my entire life. A grace is an unmerited favor, and her love is something that I didn't earn. Her love is greater than silver or gold to me and causes me to be humble and unworthy. My heart must first of all be emptied of all the sorrow that the Great Spirit has put there just a few weeks ago. While I was away, the murderer and robber Juan Garcia killed my wife. Since then, I've had no one to love to fill the emptiness that my love for her had in my life. Remorse sits in its place, for I wasn't there to protect her. Memories of her and of her ways and longing for her only torment me. My heart is full of mourning, but unlike you, it's not things that I need to destroy, but it's time that I need to temper my memories so that love for another may anoint my heart with gladness again. Until I can stop mourning, I cannot find a place in my heart for another, even one so pretty in form and beauty as Causes to Laugh.

"There are other things in my heart that shouldn't be there. There is anger and revenge against Juan Garcia for what he did. I've prayed to my God for the sin which I harbor there, and I've found refuge under his wings. I'm also praying that he'll forgive me of my shortcomings and help me that I might love again. Causes to Laugh, I can't marry with all of this in my heart. Please forgive me!" I said.

Amos spoke and the faces of my Indian friends showed sympathy and sadness. The change that came on Causes to Laugh was remarkable. Her face radiated her forgiveness, and her love to me was very clear and plain. A smile changed her distraught face to one of happiness and pleasure. Causes to Laugh spoke very softly, and Amos smiled. Wolf Fang sat, shaking his head in agreement with me.

"She forgives you, Boss! So does Chief Wolf Fang!"

The meeting was over, and I perceived that my case had been well-stated.

So, I was restored to good favor with the family and especially Causes to Laugh. She was around me constantly, carrying my water and bringing my food. She was very happy and showed it, and her happiness caused me to notice her more. She was just about as pretty a girl as I'd seen. I found myself comparing her with Melody. I need to get away from this. Amos and I need to get home, and soon.

THE BISON HUNT

My decision was made to get back to the ranch. That afternoon, a brave rode into the village, and he seemed beside himself with excitement. He rode straight to Wolf Fang and Red Hand and pointed toward the north. Amos stood smiling as the entire village laughed and danced.

"What's all the excitement?" I asked.

"That's one of Wolf Fang's scouts, and he's found bison," said Amos.

I understood then what this meant, for a lot of their heavy clothing came from the beast. They enjoyed the meat and used the skins in various ways.

"Boss, we'll have to make a decision right away, for the whole village will be moving to be nearer the bison herd," he said.

"I'd like to be in the hunt, and let's stay for another week anyway," I said.

The next morning, the women were up before dawn taking down wigwams and piling their poles in various areas. The huge bison rugs that covered the wigwam was rolled up and tied on long poles, which in turn were attached to horses. Everyone was in a happy, festive spirit. We were off with Wolf Fang and Red Hand leading the way.

Amos and I were back among most of the braves. That many people stirred up dust that would be seen for miles. Scouts kept going out, and then would report when they returned to Wolf Fang. My mind went back to Gettysburg, when Jeb Stewart failed to report to Lee. The general didn't know fully where the main body of the Northern soldiers was, for Stewart was his eyes. The failure of Stewart in scouting contributed greatly to our loss of the battle.

●

Wolf Fang knew where the bison were. His scouts were busy, and in our third day, Wolf Fang stopped and gave orders to his tribe. We were on the edge of the grass lands, and apparently the bison herd was near.

"The Coldwater River is just to the south of us," declared Amos. "This may well be where Wolf Fang will want to put his village."

The chief called a halt near the river, and there the activity began as everything was unpacked. It wasn't long before the wig-wams were up. The horse herd was down river from us and well-guarded. More scouts were sent out and returned with additional information.

"Wolf Fang said that the bison herd was about one mile north of us," said Amos.

I got out my guns and checked them over and put my belts of cartridges across my shoulders. I went to the chief and showed him which boxes of cartridges to use in the ten-gauge, and also took heavy loads for Red Hand's shot gun. I told them that they might tear great holes in the pelt of the bison, and it might be better not to use the shot guns for fear of ruining the hides. Since I was supposed to be a great hunter, Causes to Laugh got two friends to follow me to clean and cut up the meat. Wolf Fang had a different plan for me.

Amos came to me and said, "Boss, we don't know where other tribes are and it may well be that once we've made a kill and have cut up the meat that a neighboring tribe might want to stage a raid on us."

I thought about it and agreed, and we talked to Wolf Fang about it.

"My scouts have reported a large tribe about ten miles from us, but on the other side of the herd. We'll be very wary once we've made our kill," he said. "I want you to be a shooter," he said. "Get your gun and come with me."

We went into the high grass and found a small hill overlooking the herd.

"Many times, they'll pay no attention to falling bison or to the sound of a gun. Just keep on shooting till they move," said Amos.

"Which do you want killed? The bulls or the females?" I asked.

"Both," he said, "start now! Shoot them right behind the front leg."

I aimed and shot twenty-five times, and twenty animals lay on the ground. I could see that my rifle was not heavy enough. I'd hit all twenty-five times, but the shock of the hit was not completely knocking them down. The huge animals just stood there and gave me excellent targets. I loaded and reloaded, and still they didn't move off.

"It is enough," said Wolf Fang.

The ground was covered with dead animals, and my gun barrel was hot to the touch. The braves stood looking in awe at the piles of dead animals that were heaped together.

"Amazing, Boss," said Amos.

The whole tribe converged on the downed bison. The hunting was over, and the work began. Everyone was smiling at me. Old "Yellow Boy" had done its thing and I hadn't moved but a step or two from where I started shooting. Red Hand brought a beating bison heart to me and offered it. Amos had a raw liver in his hand and began to tear the flesh with his teeth. Vomit came up into my throat, and I just moved back from the villagers. They were very frantically butchering, skinning, and eating the raw flesh. I got my pack horses and hauled cut portions of meat back to the village.

It was a long day, but every bison that was killed was cleaned, and by the end of day, all that could be seen of the great slaughter were the dark circles of blood where they'd fallen. There would be much dancing, and the drums would beat as the village rejoiced in the kill. Wolf Fang had sent out scouts to keep watch on activity in the other village.

•

I wasn't on guard, for others were scheduled for that. I was awakened from my sleep by a nearby movement and reached for my gun. In the early morning light, I saw Amos. He had his hand about to shake me, when I awoke. He held his finger to his lips for silence. There were a good seventy braves slipping across the lower ground toward our village. A quail whistled, and one of our guards was warning that the enemy was approaching.

Out of the grass rose all the braves of our village; Wolf Fang's ten-gauge boomed and Red Hand's shot gun blasted. I began to shoot as fast as I could, and Amos joined me. The enemy was taken completely by surprise, and it was slaughter again, except this time it was human beings who died. The Kiowa screamed their war cries and followed the shooting with arrows. The village braves surged forward with war clubs and knives. The battle was over quickly, and the enemy fled.

That night, our warriors sat around the camp fires and told their stories. Many bloody scalps hung at various wigwams, and the old chief told of the surprise the ten-gauge had caused and the number it'd killed. Red Hand smiled as he held up the twelve-gauge gun and pointed to five bloody scalps attached to his spear.

Together, we worked for a full week, but the village had all they needed and moved their camp to the other side of the river. It was time for me to go home, and I told them so. Causes to Laugh came with tears in her eyes.

"Do you still mourn?" she asked.

I looked at her and reached for her, and she came willingly into my arms. I kissed her, and it thrilled me to no end; but I needed to get home, where I could think about this situation with a calm mind.

HOMEWARD BOUND

"Amos, we're out of here!" I cried.

Braves saluted us and Wolf Fang and Red Hand indicated for us to go in peace. There was a dense overcast, and the sun was hidden.

We crossed the Coldwater, North and South Palo Duro, where the weather took a turn for the worse. Bits of sleet started to fall, and the wind turned cold and was biting like a knife. I went to my pack and found something I didn't know I had: a seasoned bison robe. Causes to Laugh had seen that I didn't have a heavy coat and had given me hers. I gladly put it on over my deerskin jacket, and then I thought about her. They were knee deep in new bison pelts when we left. She gave me one of her seasoned robes. Bless her! Was that robe ever warm!

"Her half sister is just like her," Amos said, thinking of his wife.

He took my slicker and put it over his deer jacket.

"There's my overcoat in there too, if you want it," I said.

The bison robe hung all the way to my moccasins. We both got down from our horses, and he got my overcoat from the pack horse. I put on my boots. We dreaded crossing the Canadian River and hoped there was no ice. Crossing was not as hard as we dreaded. Just to the south of the river, we came across several shod horse prints. Amos got off his horse and knelt down to study them.

"Looks like the U.S. army has been along here. They're trailing some unshod horses. Cavalry prints aren't over a few hours old, I would say," Amos reported.

"Show me how to tell that," I requested.

He got back off his horse and pointed to the unshod horse prints.

"You see these were made yesterday, for they've little frozen crystals in them and we know that it froze last night. Notice that the shod tracks have no frozen crystals, so they were made this morning. The unshod tracks have a lot of ice crystals that have accumulated all morning. The shod horses have some, but not much. They can't be more than a couple hours old," he instructed.

"Well, I'll be!" I said in awe.

"Twenty-five soldiers and five Indians!" he added.

We picked up speed and were about a mile from the ranch when we saw the troopers.

"Looks like that lieutenant," said Amos.

"I believe you're right. Wonder who he's after? You don't think it's our Apache band, do you?"

I could see the ranch looked just fine and there was smoke coming from the chimneys. Horses were in the paddocks, and cattle dotted the fields. A sense of pride filled my chest as I looked at the beauty of the entire area.

"Lord, thank you," I whispered.

"Halt," commanded the lieutenant.

The troop was waiting for us. We all greeted one another.

"How are you, lieutenant?" Then I saw the double bars on his shoulder. "Err, excuse me, captain."

We both smiled.

"Congratulations," I said with a smile.

"Every time that I head this way, it seems that we've a Northerner," he quipped.

"You just want our hospitality again. Southern hospitality is hard to beat."

"The colonel was truly upset when you brought those cattle by and he heard what had happened to your wife and crew. I've been in the field looking for that special bunch of Apache. We caught up with them once and sent five of our wounded back to the fort. Killed three of them, but missed Garcia; however, he was seen in that bunch that we've been following. Think you can help us with some supplies?"

"Come on! Let's get in some warm buildings. Man, that wind is cold, and I believe it's winding up for a blizzard," I said.

We were met by two cowboys who were on sentry duty.

"Hello, Boss. Hi, Amos!" they both said. "Hello, Captain."

They turned and nodded to the troop and waved at some that they remembered.

"Seen any Apache this morning?" asked the captain.

"We saw four riders, but they avoided the ranch and hit for the hills there," said a cowboy.

"You guys look about frozen. Come on in," I said to my sentries.

Their faces lit up, and they nodded their thanks. Rex was standing in front of the bunkhouse and greeted the captain, Amos, and me.

"Figured you guys would be coming in," he said to the troopers. "You brought that Northerner with you, so you can enjoy our southern hospitality," said Rex.

We looked at each other and smiled.

"Just what we told them." I grinned.

"Get down and put your horses in that barn. There's plenty of good hay, oats, and some corn in that corn crib. Horses can use corn to warm them in this weather," Rex stated.

Several of the cowboys came out of the bunkhouse and greeted the captain and various soldiers. The old first sergeant yelled that the troop was dismissed as soon as the horses were seen to. The cook came out of the hacienda and greeted the army cook. He counted noses, and they went back inside where he introduced the army cook to Erma. Erma didn't stand around, but came running to greet Amos and me. She got a good hugging from both of us, and we introduced her to the captain and the sergeant. We went in to assign bunks, while Erma and the cooks got to work preparing supper for everyone.

The wind howled and the snow fell and drifted. *I would hate to be those Indians out in this without shelter,* I thought. I went out to check on Ebony and my grulla mare. I rubbed Ebony down, though someone had already done it, but I wanted to show the black stallion that I loved him. I felt a need for the love that I had with Delight. Boy, how she loved this place, and there in the runway of the barn was the surrey covered with a blanket. Hanging on a peg was Delight's side saddle.

I sat down a minute and put my head in my hands and visualized her blond hair and those beautiful green eyes and her dimple. I suddenly had tears in my eyes. *Oh, how I wish she were here. Causes to Laugh, I'm still in mourning!*

The storm lasted for three days; then warm weather came, and the storm was gone. The snow had been deep, but now the fields were standing in water from melted snow, and there were large puddles in the soft fields. Rex sent out his cowboys to check on cattle and horses. We'd weathered this storm much better than the last one, for we found no dead cattle.

"The colonel told me to tell you that we'll be needing another thousand head of cattle in the spring. His guess is about the middle of March. Telegraph us when you're ready to make the drive, and we'll meet you with a detail. Indians seem to be more restless, and we try to discourage them with more troops. We've a totally black troop on up north, but they appear to be good at fighting the Indian," said the Captain. "Thanks for the added supplies. I'll make a report of it, and you'll be replenished when you deliver the cattle. This storm has washed out all tracks of the Indians we were trailing. Our patrol is headed back for the fort."

My thoughts went back to the Apache they'd been trailing, and I wondered how they'd survived. For a week I stayed close to the ranch and fed a lot of hay during that period, but the cowboys had put up plenty. Rex sent crews out looking for more wild horses, and many more cattle were found. Most of them carried our brand, and many calves were discovered among our cattle. Some cows had dropped their calves during the storm, but the calves seemed sturdy and strong.

"We'll need to brand them before long," said Rex. "I see a lot of new horses that've been bred and born here this year. You want them branded also, or will the army be buying them?"

"I don't know. The captain said nothing about more horses right now. Hold off on branding horses for the time being," I said.

I COME TO MATT'S AID

"I see the surrey is in the barn. We have a couple horses trained to pull it, don't we? I'm going to town and will follow the cook when he goes for supplies. I'll take the surrey and let Ebony take a rest."

"Boss, you be careful taking that surrey to town, as they're having dances in there now. It might give you an idea to take one of those pretty town girls to a dance," chided Rex.

"That's an idea!"

I laughed. It was far from my mind, for I felt melancholy. I put my Winchester in the surrey along with my gun belts. You just never knew when they'd be needed. As I started down the trail, I belted on my six-gun and tied it to my leg. The road still had some puddles, so I was paying attention to my driving. The surrey handled nicely, and I sat back to make myself more comfortable. The horse wanted to trot, and I gave it some rein.

The town limits were just ahead when I heard gun shots. They were coming from the Last Chance Saloon. I pulled up, tied my horse to a hitching rack, and picked up my Winchester and walked to the swinging bats of the saloon. It took a second for my eyes to get accustomed to the darkened room. I saw someone I'd seen before and recognized as one of the four men who I had trouble with at the restaurant. He was pointing a gun. My eyes followed his pointing gun and I saw the back of Matt standing, looking away from him. My Winchester came to a steady point and I yelled, "Hold it."

The man with the gun whirled and fired; the bullet hit the swinging bats, and pieces and splinters of wood stung my hand.

The "Golden Boy" jumped in my hands and the man was flung backward from the impact of my bullet.

"It's me, Matt," I yelled, in case he was in doubt who was behind him at the door.

I came into the room and kicked the revolver away from the man lying on the floor. I stooped down and felt his pulse and found that he had none. He was dead; shot dead center through the heart. I picked up his gun and stood back to back with Matt.

"Thanks, Tom. I appreciate your help," he said.

There were two men lying dead on the floor. One had on a ranger star, and the other one was another of the four men I'd seen at the restaurant.

"Turn around," Matt said to a large, unshaven giant of a man.

Matt slipped a set of handcuffs on him and then bent over the ranger. I recognized Matt's deputy as the young ranger that I'd met in the restaurant that knew Melody. He'd been shot through the side, and the bullet had exited his other side. Matt felt for a pulse and shook his head.

"Boy, I hate that," he said. "He was such a good kid." Matt turned toward the men standing at the bar. "Okay, who saw it?" he asked.

A smiling gambler said, "Your man came in here and pulled on Robbie there, and he just was too slow. When will you law men understand that Robbie is the greatest? Your deputy pulled and had his gun half out when Robbie pulled in self-defense and had to kill him."

"Did you see what happened when I fired?" I asked.

"Didn't see that," he smirked.

"I saw it, and you shot that man just as he was aiming to kill the ranger," spoke up one customer. "You yelled for him to hold it, but he fired at you before you shot him."

"Thanks," I said.

Matt took a pencil and wrote down the witness's name.

"Come with me; I need a statement from you."

Matt took his prisoner on down to the jail, and the witness followed. The witness made a statement, which Matt wrote down and had the witness sign it. Matt then locked Robbie in a cell.

"Did you see that your deputy was shot from his side and not from the front?" I asked Matt.

He nodded that he had.

"This won't hold up. I have friends," said Robbie.

Matt hung the keys on a peg and turned to me.

"That was a close one. You about lost old Dad there." He smiled. "I need to get my deputy cared for and arrangements made for him. I believe you'd met him, hadn't you? He was Ranger Wayne Crosby and a local boy, and it'll kill his parents. I need to get our undertaker to take care of those other two also. I'll be back in an hour. Wait for me, will you, or do you want to come along?" asked Matt. I told him I'd wait at the office. He came back to the office looking tired and despondent.

"That boy was all the Crosby's had! They lost two sons in the war," he said.

"I'm sure sorry, Matt, as he sure seemed like a good boy," I remarked.

Matt suddenly looked very tired and weary. He was sick of the whole setup, and he told me some of his feelings.

"Tom, you know we had a constitutional convention at Austin in April 1866, and in June, in our general election, we elected James W. Throckmorton to be the governor of this state. July 30, 1867, he was removed from office and General P.H. Sheridan replaced him and was made Commander of the Fifth Military District, with headquarters in New Orleans. His district covers this area, and we have a general rebellion against what he is trying to do. The clan has really been active, and there have been several people found dead; I believe it to be the result of their hatred of Sheridan and some of the blue bellies that've come into the state. Poor Wayne is the direct result of something in which he'd no part," Matt said.

"Let's go get a cup of coffee," I said.

Melody stared at me when I entered the restaurant.

"Welcome, stranger," she said.

I hugged her slightly and she smiled. She looked at Matt and said hi to him; then she turned to me.

"Where have you been, Tom?"

"Been out in the wilds with the Kiowa, hunting and enjoying

myself," I said. "Trying to forget a lot, but having trouble in doing that," I continued.

"I see you came in your surrey," she said. "What'll you have?"

She waited, watching me over her note pad.

"Coffee and a piece of your pie," I said. "I hope to eat this one in peace!"

"And you, Matt?' she asked.

"Give me the same," was his answer.

"Well, Matt, what's happening? Does this killing leave you alone in your office?" I asked.

Melody was back with the pie and coffee.

"Oh, I'm so sorry; the cook just told me what happened. That poor Wayne! He was such a good kid!"

She looked very distressed.

"I still have a couple that I can call on if I need a posse. Still have the livery man. What would I do without him? This Robbie is fast with a gun, and he'll take advantage if he can. Your killing that carpetbagger won't be useful to you. They've money and will have Robbie out of jail in a few days. He and his friends will come looking for both of us. Houston must get me some help, as a lot of this is getting into politics, and we're still fighting the war in the political arena," Matt said, almost to himself.

"Also, there's something going on which my own people are trying to keep from me. It's called the Ku-Klux Klan or 'KKK' for short. They're simply a group of white Southerners trying to fight back, and they're doing it by terror methods. There are times when they'll need the rangers to take a fight against my own friends, but we need justice, not terrorism. Some of my friends have become my enemies because I don't take a stand with them and wear a white sheet. I won't do it. I can't," Matt continued, almost beside himself.

"Matt, you've a friend here, and have my guns if you need them. I'll get a room at the hotel so I can be near," I said.

"No, Tom. Bess would run me off if I let you do that. Our home is your home. You know that. You just come on over, and remember supper is at 6:oo."

"Matt, I just brought enough clothes to stay a few days, so I'll need to send back for some more. My cook'll be here tomorrow, and I can send for some clothes through him. What's your plan?" I asked.

"The judge'll be here next week, and I hope I can keep Robbie in jail until then. Everyone seems to be organized against us rangers. They'll try to make something out of what you did, believe me. I tell you, they are ruthless," said Matt. "I'm headed for home, as I want to have your name in the pot for tonight. Bess will be glad to see you," said Matt. "Want to go?"

"I want to talk with Melody," I said, and Matt left.

"Melody, more coffee!" I called.

She brought the coffee pot to the table and sat down opposite me. She had a cup and filled both of them with coffee.

"I need a break," she said. "Thanks for telling me about Bess needing someone to care for. She's like a mother to me, and that's something I never had. Loving each other has been good for both of us. She's such a fine woman."

I TAKE MELODY TO A DANCE

"Melody, you don't have any fun in life. You're too young to just work, work, work. I hear that they have dances here now, and I came to town especially to take you to the dance tomorrow night."

Her face turned as red as a beet.

"Oh, Tom, I've so wanted to go, but I don't have a good dress. I'm asked almost every week, but by no one that I'll go with. There're very few decent men in this area. We lost the cream of the crop in that terrible war."

She sat there thinking. Finally, she turned and looked at me.

"If I can find a dress, you've a date." She laughed.

I had a ten dollar bill in my hands.

"Here's for the coffee and a new dress," I said.

"Oh, I couldn't do that." Then she thought a minute. "But I will."

Her lovely blue eyes were turned on me, and they danced with happiness. I saw the dark eyes of Causes to Laugh, and then there were the green eyes of Delight, as if they were standing over us.

"I'll pick you up at 7:00," I said, and squeezed her hand. "I'm looking forward to it."

The town looked the same. I stared with sadness as I passed the bank where Delight had worked. Matt's home looked the same. I tied my horse and buggy to the horse rail at the front of the house.

I hugged mother Bess and she clung to me in the parlor of their home. She held me at arm's length and said, "Let me look at you! Don't you look handsome?"

"Bess, you look so much better than the last time I saw you," I added.

"It's that Melody; it's as if we had another daughter. Tom, she's kind beyond her years. She's had such a difficult life, you know."

"Yes, she's a sweet young lady and a hard worker! I feel that she works too much, and I plan to do something about it."

Bess showed a quizzical expression.

"What do you mean? Are you going to take her away from the restaurant?"

"No, Bess. I've invited her to the dance tomorrow night," I corrected her.

"And she said she'd go?" asked Bess, and a light of joy came to her face. "It'll make her so happy. I must help her get ready, if she'll let me. Tom, the poor thing has no clothes."

"Sweet Bess, that's all been arranged!" I added.

She led me into the kitchen, which was filled with pleasant cooking aromas. I followed her to hug her again. Matt came through the house and stood looking on. He walked up and put his arms around us both, and we just hugged and smiled.

Dinner was excellent, for Bess was such a good cook. Around the table we discussed a variety of subjects concerning Melody and my dance invitation. Matt and I talked about the trouble at the Last Chance Saloon when Bess was out of the room.

Bess was deeply distressed over the death of Wayne Crosby. Matt didn't tell her of my intervention and the killing that followed. After dinner, as Bess did the dishes, Matt and I retired to the living room.

"Matt, since you've lost Wayne Crosby, who'll be watching your back? I want to help you, as you don't seem to have anyone that wants to step up. My guns will help you to bring justice here."

"I need to deputize you so that everything will be legal. Lift your hand and swear after me," said Matt.

I took the oath, and he pinned a ranger star on me.

"This is one job that I never dreamed I'd have," I said as I looked at the star. "What will be my first assignment?"

He grinned.

"I'll figure something out."

I slept in Delight's old bedroom. The next morning, we all had breakfast, and I put on the badge and followed Matt around town to get acquainted with the area. Before the day was up, I knew most of the streets and alleys. I'd been in all three saloons, but the Last Chance appeared to be the hangout of the troublemakers. There were about a half dozen mean-looking characters drinking and cursing in there.

It was time to get ready for the dance. I had my best suit with me, so I prepared by bathing, shaving, and shining my boots. I was looking forward to giving Melody a good time. She'd been in my mind a lot lately. I brushed my horse while I still had light and took the surrey to the restaurant. The cook and a waitress looked me over as I walked in.

"She'll be out in a minute!"

I sat at a table and waited for her, and I felt like there were was several pair of eyes summing me up. I looked out the window and watched several townspeople walk by.

Someone cleared their throat lightly, and I turned and arose at the same time. The chair fell over backwards, and I tried in vain to catch it. Melody stood there with a look of glee on her face, and then she could hold it no longer. She giggled, and then laughed out loud. She was joined by others from the kitchen area; I felt like a school boy, but had to join with them all in laughter. She was looking me over, and it was my turn to admire her. She was worth all I'd been through, for she truly was a beautiful girl, and she'd chosen well with her new dress. The dress was a pale blue and trimmed in white ruffles at her throat. The color of the dress accentuated the color of her eyes and the light brown of her hair.

"I'm sorry, but I've no flowers, as it's the wrong time of the year," I said.

I held her coat for her as she moved gracefully into each sleeve. She had a blue ribbon in her hair. Her lovely blue eyes were smiling. Could it possibly be that I could enjoy three of the most beautiful girls that God had created? This girl has uncanny beauty and charm! I summed it all up. She had a small purse, which she shifted to her left hand as she slipped her arm though mine.

"Good night," she said.

There was a chorus of "good nights," from the kitchen. She giggled again, and I waved a hand at the unseen group.

I helped her into the surrey and clucked the horse into motion. I had an iron weight on a strap that I fastened to the bridle when I parked the surrey at the dance hall. I helped her down, and we went into the building. The music was being played by a local group; their music wasn't the greatest, but we could dance to it. I swung her onto the floor, and for a minute or so, she and I were the only couple dancing. I'd mastered dancing when I was in the army and became a first lieutenant. I attended several balls during my military experience, and I wondered where she'd learned. She was good, so we made a graceful pair as we glided around the floor. Several were watching and some didn't know me, so they were wondering who I was.

I held her close and looked down into her blue eyes.

"Oh, Tom, you dance so well!"

Around and around the floor we glided. I sure hoped that she was enjoying this as much as I. The music ended, and there was a flock of men standing at my elbow.

"May I have the next dance?" was repeated several times.

She knew several of them and took out a little book and wrote a few names in it. I stood there realizing what a popular girl she was, and I was a little jealous, but I was happy for her.

A rather nice-looking young man took her in his arms as the music began and moved with her out onto the floor. I walked toward a wall which was lined with couples. I knew no one, so I stood with my hands in my pocket.

I'm the odd one out, I thought.

The music ended and another young man approached her and said, "I believe this is my dance."

She smiled at him and then at me, and off they went. There was a large bowl of punch with small glasses to one side. I suddenly felt I needed to do something, so I reached for a cup.

"Here, let me help you," a young lady said.

I took the cup and expressed my thanks to her.

"You're Tom McDowell, aren't you?"

I turned to see a blond haired girl smiling at me. She was pretty, but nothing to compare with Delight and Melody, nor Causes to Laugh.

"Yes," I said. "May I ask your name?"

"I'm Cathy Duncan." When she saw that the name hadn't registered with me, she said, "Robert Duncan is my dad."

Still, I was slow to show recognition.

"My dad is owner of the bank here."

"Oh, of course. I'm sorry, Cathy!"

I turned toward her and saw that, indeed, she was an attractive girl. Her dress showed that a pretty penny had gone into its creation.

"I knew Delight when she worked for Dad. Oh, Tom, it was so terrible. I am so sorry for you. Everyone thought so highly of her," Cathy said with true regret.

"Thanks very much," I said.

I looked back to Melody. Someone was cutting in on her partner. She didn't want to dance with this new guy, but he brushed her partner away and seized her.

"Oh, that man, that awful man!" spoke Cathy. "That's Jody and he's been drinking."

Melody kept pulling, trying to break away. I left Cathy and walked onto the floor and approached the struggling couple. I took his arm and twisted it back behind him. A look of pain and anger came into his face.

"I don't think that the lady wants to dance with you," I said.

With my free arm, I reached for the ranger badge and pinned it on my shirt pocket. He whirled with an oath, and I let lose of his arm. He saw the badge and hesitated.

"Can't a guy have fun with his girl without you rangers sticking your nose into it?"

His voice was slurred from drink.

"Don't believe she is your girl, friend," I said. "I believe I brought her myself."

I took Melody in my arms and danced her away from him. People that overheard my remark laughed, and it was like putting kindling on a fire. His face reddened.

His face was a dark red and his eyes bulged.

"Who is that card?" I asked Melody.

"Tom, he's one of those Northerners, and he'll cause trouble for you. He causes me a lot of headaches at work. His name is Jody Williams and he is a friend of Robbie that Matt has in jail. He claims he's the fastest man in Texas with a six-gun. He thinks Robbie isn't as good as he."

I looked over at him and there was no gun visible. Guns had to be checked at the door, and the new local marshal was watching over them.

"Oh, Tom, I heard that the carpetbaggers were causing trouble, but I hoped they'd let us have some fun at our own dances," she whispered.

Jody Williams had found some sympathizers, and they were standing around him along one wall of the room. He watched us dance, and I could see him working himself up. The music stopped and Jody was headed our way.

I whispered to Melody, "Go powder your nose."

She stepped back and headed to a corner of the room. He tried to follow her, but I cut him off. He swung a vicious blow at me, which I stepped under and caught him coming in with a hard right cross. It sounded like a sledge hammer hitting a fallen tree. He was thrown backward and slid across the floor into the crowd that was following him. They stopped and looked at me and then at poor Jody, who was out for the night. There was an angry cry that came from them, but they didn't advance. The marshal approached and told them to behave. They picked up Jody and turned toward the door, and when they were gone, all the town residents applauded my activity.

"You can expect trouble over this," said the marshal. "You're Tom McDowell? I'm Marshal Jon McGinnis. The mayor just hired me a week ago, and I look forward to working with Matt. I see you're a ranger too, so maybe we can watch one another's back. When did you get your star?" he asked.

"Yesterday after I backed up Matt at the Last Chance," I answered.

"Yes, I heard about that, and I may need you and Matt to do the same with me. Some of those guys from the North are determined to show us who won the war, and now they plan to rule. They are riff-raff, and they know it, but have a couple of really good gunmen that they've brought in here from Kansas," he said.

"We have to stop this before it gets out of hand and look for them to bring in the Federal government. We need to have witnesses who will stand up and testify to the truth or else we'll all go down. Whether you're a ranger or a town marshal may not make a bit of difference. Now is the time for the entire town to stand up. Did you hear the town people applaud when the carpetbaggers left the dance tonight? That also was for you standing up like you did. I sure hope that Jody lives through the night. That was really one stiff punch, and I believe you hit him right between the eyes. I bet he'll not see light for a week. His eyes will be swollen shut," he chuckled.

The band had started playing, and the dancers were moving onto the floor. A young man was dancing with Melody, and she seemed to be enjoying it. I watched her and smiled. I hope this fighting didn't ruin her evening. I watched her as she let another half dozen men dance with her. I looked up Cathy, and found that she danced well and was light on her feet. I danced two dances with her and went back to Melody.

"When is it my turn again?" I asked.

"Now and every dance the rest of the night if you wish" she said with a sparkle in her eye. "Your hand looks swollen. Poor Jody he won't eat for a week. You hit him right in the teeth, didn't you?"

"The marshal disputes you, for he said I got him right between the eyes."

I got my gun from the marshal and told Melody to stay in the building until I found all things were clear. Everything looked clear, and I had my bison coat to cover us, so we rode around for a while. It was a beautiful night, and the moon was full. My mind went to Delight, but it didn't stay there long. Melody cuddled up next to me to keep warm, and we pulled the bison robe higher. Causes to Laugh wouldn't appreciate my using her gift that way. I smiled. *How in the world will I ever decide which one is for me? I need a full time woman and I need to settle down*, I thought.

"In spite of Jody trying to ruin the night, it turned out to be a night that I always will remember. Thanks, Tom. It was thoughtful of you."

She kissed me full upon the lips and moved when I wanted more. She was at the door of the restaurant and then threw me another kiss and went inside.

I put the horse in the warm stable and went inside where Matt and Bess were half asleep in the parlor. Were they waiting up for me?

"We couldn't sleep and were wondering how you got along with Melody. Tom, she's like a second daughter to us, and we both love her so very much. Bess mothers her to no end," said Matt.

"And what about you, dear husband? She has you all tied up and in knots just like Delight did," chided Bess.

"Both of them were named well. Delight was truly a delight to me and Melody, well, she causes a melody in my heart too," I said.

"Boy, I'm worn out. I'm for bed," Matt whispered.

He picked up his shoes and, yawning, went toward their bedroom.

"Me, too," Bess and I said in unison.

"Matt, I had some trouble at the dance tonight, but it really didn't amount to much," I continued.

"Oh, no!" exclaimed Bess.

Matt turned back to me.

"What kind of trouble, Tom?" he asked.

"Jody Williams was drunk and tried to make Melody dance with him," I answered.

"And?" he asked.

"He'll have trouble getting his eyes open in the morning." I grinned.

"He's had that coming for some time, and I'm glad that you administered justice," Matt remarked with a smile.

"I put my ranger star on, but it made no difference. He swung at me and missed. I thought if he tried to pursue the fight, I'd arrest him for assaulting an officer," I smiled.

"Good thinking, Tom. I can't keep my eyes open, so we'll talk about it in the morning," Matt said, and he headed to bed.

I slept in the same bed that Delight and I shared when we were visiting her folks. I laid there for an hour or so, thinking first of Delight and then of Melody. Causes to Laugh and my brief problem with her caused me to be uneasy. I'm sure that she'd argue that I was no longer in mourning for Delight. *Perhaps she is right.* I thought. *Still, I think of Delight often. She'll never be forgotten.*

●

Matt, Bess, and I had an early breakfast, and I went out to check on my surrey horse. I needed a saddle horse, but I only had the surrey. I decided to go ahead and drive my surrey around to help Matt with his rounds. Several of the townspeople had heard of the fight at the dance, and they were showing their appreciation when they met me. There were several who waved at me and several took their hats off to me, and I returned the salute.

I went into the Last Chance Saloon, but it appeared too early for their crowd. A lone gambler was at a table playing solitaire.

"Hello, Ranger! I hear that you stuck your foot into the local trouble last night. Jody swears that he'll shoot you on sight." He smiled. "That's when he can see you. He has a steak on each eye, and his nose is broken. He has a couple of gunslinger friends from Kansas who'll be picking a fight with you as soon as they can. I'm telling you this to warn you. I hate to see a ranger shot down, as I'm from Texas, you know. I believe that you've a hand stacked against you, though," he said.

"I'm surprised, for I heard you speaking to Matt yesterday. I'm sure that Ranger Crosby didn't have much of a chance against Robbie."

"Not so loud! These walls have ears. There were others that saw it, and I didn't want to step up when that guy spoke out to tell how it really happened. If I was you, I'd keep him out of sight until he can testify against Robbie. Believe me, those Kansas gunfighters are good. Since I'm talking and there's just you and me here, there's someone from town that's back of these carpetbaggers and is financing them. Several gunmen, including Robbie, two from Kansas, Jody and the four that you fought at the restaurant, needed food and lodging and someone to pay for their gambling and booze. .

Watch for someone who has money and has prestige." Said the gambler

He turned back to his game as the bartender moved toward us.

"Thanks," I whispered, as I left the room.

Later that afternoon, standing in front of the jail, I told Matt of my conversation with the gambler. Matt listened and considered what I'd told him.

"I think that I'll be able to tell who'll get some of this abandoned land when it comes to push and shove at the end. Their financial backer will need to show his hand when he puts his name on the title of the land he is stealing through this carpetbagger laws," Matt said.

RANGERS RELIEVED OF DUTY AND MELODY GETS A SPECIAL JOB

"Matt, here's a telegram for you from headquarters, and it doesn't look good for you guys," said the marshal.

Matt read the telegram, and as he did, he had to sit down.

"Since we haven't yet been accepted back into the United States of America, our status as peace officers is no more. No funds, no job, and no authority to hold Robbie. Tom, you and I are out of jobs, and I never had the authority to swear you into an organization that doesn't exist."

He took his star and laid it on the desk as he spoke. Matt almost staggered for he was about to the end of his rope.

"I knew that Texas had voted down the 13th and 14th amendments to the Constitution," I said. "I've been away from papers, and have no idea just what's coming off. I see now why that one thousand dollar reward wasn't paid to me."

"What a blow! It has a lot to do with these carpetbagger laws," Matt said. "I owe five hundred on my house, and have to tell Bess that I'm unemployed. Oh, marshal, are you going to hold Robbie?"

The marshal took Matt's keys and told Matt he would prosecute Robbie. I sat in the surrey completely stunned.

"I was about to wire Houston, as I haven't been paid for six months," said Matt. "I'm destitute. I owe the bank; I owe the

Livery stable; I owe for groceries. This will kill Bess." Matt walked home to tell Bess.

My thoughts went to Matt and Bess. I could use them both at the ranch. He'd make a good ramrod to help Rex, and she could help Erma with the house. Sure, why not? I followed Matt to the house where I found Bess weeping and Matt sitting with his face in his hands.

"Matt, if this had to happen, then it couldn't have come at a better time," I stated. "I need a ramrod to help Rex at the ranch. You'd take the place vacated when Paul was killed. Bess, I need a woman to run the hacienda and work with Erma."

"You mean that?" asked Matt. "You aren't saying that just because of these circumstances are you?"

"Matt, put the house here up for sale. I believe you can get a thousand out of it. You could pay off the five hundred, and you all come and live with me at the hacienda."

"Let Bess and me talk it over, Tom. There's Melody to think of too. I'd hate to leave her here in this town without protection. Those Northerners are mean guys."

The cook was in town with the wagon for supplies. I drilled him about things at the ranch, and he gave a good report. I told him to take the supplies on back, and then to bring two empty wagons back for Matt's furniture. I was that sure he'd take the job I'd offered. I went back to the house, and Bess was smiling, as was Matt.

"You got yourself a deal, Tom," said Matt. "And you're more than a son to us! Thanks! Can we take Melody with us?"

I was stunned, and it took a few minutes to answer.

"Do you think she'd come?" I asked. "I'll go and ask her and explain the situation to her," I said.

"Want me to come along?" asked Matt.

"Oh, for goodness sakes, Matt, use your head!" called Bess.

•

I drove the surrey to the restaurant. It was mid-morning, and the place was empty. Melody was in the cook's area, but heard the door open. I seated myself as she came with her pad.

"You're hungry this time of day? What'll you have?" she said, smiling.

"I would like to take a very pretty blue-eyed waitress home with me," I said.

"Yes, and so would Jody Williams," she kidded back.

"But Melody, I mean it."

Her mouth dropped open. I then told her about the rangers closing down and Matt having no job. I told her that Matt and Bess were coming to work for me, and we all wanted her to come too. She sat down and looked very sorrowful when she thought of Matt and Bess losing their home. She smiled at me when I spoke of the remedy that I had for them.

"But Tom, what would I do?" She sat thinking.

"You could run the whole house," I said.

"You mean, I would manage such people as Erma and Bess? Oh, come on, Tom!"

"The job that I have in mind for you is to be my wife!"

The invitation was a shock to her, and she sat a moment looking at me in disbelief.

"Sweetheart, I'm waiting for an answer," I said, as I watched tears well in her eyes.

"Oh, yes, yes."

She broke down and cried. I took her in my arms and kissed her lips. I kissed away the tears. The cook was looking, and she screamed to him, "We're going to get married!"

He grinned a toothless grin and waved at the both of us.

"I want you to gather all your things, for my cook will have wagons here in the morning to move Matt and Bess. We'll have time at the hacienda to plan our marriage. Honey, I love you very much."

She came into my arms once more.

"Oh, Tom, and I love you too!"

I was sure how I felt when she said good night to me last night after the dance, and this business with Matt and Bess just pushed me in the right direction.

•

The next morning, Matt and I went to the bank. Matt was six months behind with his house payments, and the loan manager asked Matt, "How are you going to pay off your loan on your house? It's all around town that they've dissolved the rangers. Is that right, Matt?"

I spoke up and said, "I have a check for the full amount, which should make his house free and clear."

"Is Mr. Duncan in?" I continued.

"Do you have an appointment?"

"No. Just tell him that Tom McDowell is out here, and I want to see him," I spoke rather sharply.

"Yes, sir," he answered, then turned and went into the office.

"Hello, Tom. Hi, Matt. What can I do for you? My daughter, Cathy, was telling me how you handled Jody Williams the other night! It's about time that a Texan put him in his place," said Robert Duncan.

"Mr. Duncan, Matt has his house for sale, and it'd make a good investment for the bank," I said.

"Well, Tom, the bank owns it now, as he is behind $500 on that place."

"I just paid the bank's share, and I own it now with Matt. It's still for sale at $1200," I said.

"I believe that our new marshal might be interested in buying that house, come to think of it," said Mr. Duncan thoughtfully.

"Will you finance such a sale between these two law men?"

"Yes, I'll do that if the marshal is interested," said Mr. Duncan. "He makes $50 a month and is married, and appears to be a good risk."

"We'll see the marshal and get back with you," I said.

Matt looked at me a little concerned.

"That's $200 more than we were going to ask. You think it's worth it? I wouldn't want to cheat the marshal."

"Matt, Bob Duncan knows the value of every house in these parts. I'm sure that the bank has its hooks in all of them. If $1200 was too much, he would've said no to the deal." I smiled.

"Let's go and see the marshal," Matt said.

In two hours, the deal was completed and Matt had more

money than he ever had in his life: seven hundred dollars! The marshal and the bank owned Matt's house. Later that morning found Matt and Bess packing and preparing for the move. I took the surrey and drove over to the restaurant to see how Melody was getting along.

"She's in her room," the cook said, and he pointed to a room off the kitchen.

The room was small, and it was almost unbearably hot from the kitchen stove. She'd two old suitcases full of clothes and looked very ashamed of her surroundings. I knew she'd a hard time, but I'd no idea how hard. I carried her clothes to the surrey. She hugged and kissed the old cook and a second waitress.

"You've been so kind to me. I owe you so much," she said to the old cook.

There was a tear in her eye and his too.

"Oh, go on!" said the old cook. "You've been such a help to me."

"Melody, we're going shopping. The wagons aren't here yet, so I want you with a good wardrobe, and we can't get that out at the ranch," I said, looking into her eyes.

"Are you ashamed of me?" she almost whimpered.

"No, honey. I just didn't know your situation. I want you to have enough clothes to wear around the hacienda and not feel ashamed there. You'll soon be my bride. I love you!" I said with feeling.

We bought clothes, undergarments, and shoes. We bought shawls, slips, dresses, and all the things that girls need. We bought combs, toothbrushes, and perfumes. Then I asked her if any of the suitcases had clothes she didn't want, and she said, "Yes, that one." I gave it a toss and packed her clothes in four new suitcases. She was all smiles.

"I've never had that many clothes in my whole life," she said.

I turned the surrey toward Matt's. Suddenly, four horses had cut us off. One of them was Jody, and the other three were his gunmen friends. Jody's eyes were still swollen, but he managed to barely see out of them.

"You're not going to sneak out of this town without meeting my friends from Kansas, are you?" asked Jody.

I shifted my weight so that my gun would be free.

"You don't plan to start something with a woman present, do you, Jody?

"I don't think we'll have any trouble out of you. There are four of us and only one of you," sneered Jody.

Someone from behind spoke up and said, "There are six with him."

The four gunmen turned and looked into four Winchesters pointing right at them. Matt stood behind Rex and my cowboys with his pistol in his hand.

"As you were saying, Jody?" said Rex.

I smiled. All four of the gunmen froze, while Matt came and took their guns from them. He threw the guns into a water trough.

"This is not over yet," said Jody.

I got down from the surrey and slid my gun in and out of its holster. "Hand him his gun, Matt."

Jody started to squirm. Matt put it into Jody's holster. I put my gun back into my holster.

"When you're ready," I said.

He didn't move.

"My eyes make it so I can't see too well, and you're at an advantage," whined Jody.

I turned to the gunmen from Kansas.

"Any of you want to give it a shot?"

They looked down and didn't move. A crowd of people were now milling about the street. Texans enjoyed a little excitement. These town men were Southern veterans and were tired of the carpetbaggers.

"Let's lynch all four of them," said one.

Matt said, "I don't think that would look so good. The marshal may not like that at all."

"Git," I said.

All four of them looked at me and rode toward the Last Chance Saloon. Matt walked up to Jody, took his gun, and threw it into the water trough with the others.

"You ever see so-called gunmen back down like those four did?" asked Rex.

"Thanks, fellows," I said. "If you saw those Winchesters pointing at you, how'd you feel? You guys looked good to me, but mean as the devil to them."

They spoke to Melody, who was as pale as could be. She managed a smile at them.

"Fellows, she's to be my wife." It was a surprise to them all. I drove on to Matt's, and we all pitched in and loaded the furniture. We piled it high, and then started toward the ranch and a new life for Matt and Bess. I took Melody and her luggage and mine, and we rode in the surrey. My cook and Rex brought the wagons, and the cowboys watched our back trail.

MARRIED AGAIN

We drove up before the hacienda, and several cowboys came out of the bunkhouse to help with the luggage. The question in my mind was where to store Matt and Bess's furniture. I'd been thinking about the problem as Melody and I rode along from town. I could let them use one of the line shacks and padlock it good. The line shacks were so remote that very seldom anyone went near them. For the time being, we could pull the wagons into the larger barn and cover them over until the problem was solved. I wanted Matt and Bess to share the hacienda with Melody and me. There was a lot of room available, and I thought they'd enjoy living there.

I directed the cowboys to put the furniture in the big barn and cover it up so dust couldn't get to it. Bess was there to oversee the job, and Matt stood back and watched. I called them both to me and explained my problem. "My hacienda is full of my furniture, but the furniture can be rearranged so we can get your furniture into two rooms. This will be temporary until you have your own home. "

I had another thought. "Matt, Bess, there's a beautiful valley to the west of us that rises to the Cap Rock. My cattle have been in there, and we've been using it as our own. I don't know who owns it, but I believe that Don used it like I am. If we can get the deed to that land, we could cut timber off it and build you a nice home there," I said, pointing to the Cap Rock.

Bess smiled and Matt nodded agreement.

"I want you to have your own home, if you want it," I said. "You'll enjoy living at the hacienda also, as it's roomy."

The cowboys had carried Melody's luggage into the larger bedroom. My clothes were in one of the closets. She looked the room over and began to hang up her new clothing. I came in to help her, and she insisted that she needed no help. I took the empty suitcases for storage elsewhere. She was very beautiful standing there looking about. I had to hold her, and she came into my arms willingly.

"We must plan our marriage, and soon. I'll stay in the bunkhouse until then," I said.

"I don't want a big marriage, Tom. Let's just have my cook and a couple of my waitress friends out; then all the people living here. I'd like for Amos and his wife to be here too. We'll keep it small, but of course you can invite whomever you wish," she said, taking time to collect her thoughts.

"I owe the cowboys some time off and some extra money. I haven't touched the money from the last cattle drive. Christmas came and went while I was hunting with the Kiowa. There's another cattle drive due in the spring, which should bring in additional income," I said, thinking out loud.

"I need to set up some books to see just how I'm doing. I haven't been too detailed in my bookkeeping," I continued.

She sat by me on the edge of the bed. I kissed her again, and said, "Let's get married as soon as we can make arrangements with the minister."

She smiled and said, "Sounds good to me!"

I had a special meeting with my entire crew and introduced them all to Matt and Bess. I introduced them to Melody, and the cowboys all fell in love with her. Rex already knew her, and kidded me that I'd beat him to her. I remembered his kidding with Paul. No one mentioned Paul, but he was in the back of my mind, and I'm sure that Melody thought of him too. We talked about Juan Garcia and the last time that he was seen. The army detail had lost him completely because of the Northerner.

"Let's keep a couple of sentries north and south of the ranch. I don't want to get caught without the ranch having protection. Matt, since you've the experience of law enforcement, I want you to take on the security of the ranch. Rex, I want you to work the cowboys, and plan and prepare for our cattle and horse drives.

We'll service the U.S. army as long as there is a demand. I feel that the railroad will head this way in the next decade, and then things will really open up.

"Rex, I hear that you've opened that box canyon by clearing the rock from the western end, and have opened up the gates and removed the fence so the wild horses will use the canyon again. That's an excellent trap for wild horses. I want you to keep six cowboys in those line shacks to keep check on our cattle and wild horses. It'll be hard work, but keep those barns up there filled with hay.

"When Amos gets over his visit back home, I want him and his scouts to watch Juan Garcia and his Apache. I want him dead for what he did to Delight.

"Matt, the scouts will be under your jurisdiction. Also, we've a friend in the town marshal, so we need to keep in touch with him about those carpetbaggers. I want to remain friends with the Kiowa, but it'll cost us a few cows. I'd like to visit with the Apache and get acquainted with some that aren't following Garcia," I said.

•

Marriage arrangements were made with the minister, and special meals were prepared. The cook at the restaurant was invited, and Rex sent the surrey in for the cook and Melody's waitress friends. Melody and I were married, surrounded by those we loved.

Tears flooded Melody's beautiful blue eyes as she said, "I, Melody, take thee Tom, to my wedded husband, to have and to hold, till death do us part." I looked into her eyes and remembered that Delight had made the same oath last May.

I slipped the ring on her finger and Melody was Mrs. Tom McDowell. I had married twice in a year's time. Melody was an excellent lover. Her disposition was one of humility, and she considered others ahead of herself. Her past life had taught her these graces. We'd devotions as Delight and I had started. She took her love for others right into her relationship with her God, and studied her Bible as she studied her grammar and reading books. Delight had much more book learning and didn't need to study as Melody did. Melody wanted to better herself, as well as those around her.

My love for Melody grew each day. She had a strange habit of calling me "my husband" and not using my formal name. She continued to love Bess like a mother, and Matt as her dad. I too called Matt and Bess, Dad and Mom.

MELODY AND I
BECOME PARENTS

We were married six months when Melody informed me that I would be a father. She told Bess in a special way by calling her Grandmother. Both Matt and Bess were thrilled, but they weren't on cloud nine like I was. The cowboys were all thinking of themselves as Uncle. Melody added a new study to her quest for knowledge. She began to peck on the piano, and it wasn't long before she could play songs by ear. She became good overnight and would play and sing songs from memory. She knew many, for there'd been over two thousand songs written during the war. Some of the songs she sang were *We Shall Meet but We Have Missed Him*, *I'm Looking for Him Home*, *When Johnny Comes Marching Home*, and *Lorena*, as well as *The Bonny Blue Flag*. Melody would also sing *Amazing Grace* and *Sweet Hour of Prayer*, as well as other church songs. In the evening, after working hours, she'd invite her cowboys into the parlor to sing as she played. I couldn't carry a tune if it had handles on it, so I sat and enjoyed her playing and the singing.

George Cavenaugh had an excellent tenor voice and would visit us in the evenings to join with Melody in song. He loved to sing the marching song *Lorena*.

"We were evacuating Atlanta in September, 1864, and as we marched out of the city we sang *Lorena*. That song has meant a lot to me ever since," he said.

I envisioned a battered army retreating through the city singing that song. George squared his shoulders and, with tears in his eyes, he sang two of the six verses of the song written by Reverend H.D.L. Webster:

The years creep slowly by, Lorena.
Snow is on the grass again;
The sun's low down the sky, Lorena,
The frost gleams where the flowers have been;
But the heart throbs on as warmly now,
As when the summer days were nigh;
Oh! The sun can never dip so low,
      A down affection's cloudless sky.
It matters little now. Lorena,
The past is in the eternal past;
Our hearts will soon lie low, Lorena,
Life's tide is ebbing out so fast.
There is a future, oh, thank God!
Of life this is so small a part,
'Tis dust to dust beneath the sod,
But there, up there, 'tis heart to heart.

"There's a new song out, and I've heard it played by some of the guys who have been to town over the weekend. It's a comical song and was dedicated to the Honorable Thad Stevens, a Pennsylvania Congressman who advocated a mean reconstruction policy. In it were the words, 'I don't want no pardon for anything I've done.' The song had the title *O, I'm a Good Old Rebel* and was written in backwoods language and was the rebel answer to the north,'" George said. "There are at least twelve verses. Let me sing a few and Melody, maybe you can pick it up on the piano."

He sang the Texas response to the reconstruction:

O, I'm a good old Rebel,
Now that's just what I am,
For this 'Fair Land of Freedom'
I do not care ay all.
I'm glad I fit against it—
I only wish we had won,

And I don't want no pardon
For anything I've done.
I hates the Constitution,
This Great Republic too,
I hates the Freedman's Buro,
In uniforms of blue.
I hates the nasty eagle,
With all his brags and fuss,
The lyin,' thieving' Yankees,
I hates 'em wuss and wuss.
I hates the Yankee nation
And everything they do.
    I hates the Declaration
Of Independence too;
I hates the glorious Union-
'Tis dripping with our blood-
I hates their striped banner,
I fit it all I could.
I followed old mass' Robert
    For four year, near about,
    Got wounded in three places
And starved at Pint Lookout;
I cotch rheumatism
A campin' in the snow,
But I killed a chance of Yankees,
I'd like to kill some mo.'
Three hundred thousand Yankees
Is stiff in Southern dust;
We got three hundred thousand
Before they conquered us;
They died of Southern fever
And Southern steel an shot,
I wish they was three million
Instead of what we got.
I can't take up my musket
And fight 'em now no more,
But I ain't going to love 'em,

JOE WAYNE BRUMETT

Now that is sarten sure;
And I don't want no pardon
For what I was and am.
I won't be reconstructed
And I don't care a damn.

I was sitting in a chair and heard each word that George sang. I knew that there was bitterness all about me regarding the reconstruction period, but that song said it all. I wasn't prepared for Melody's reaction. Melody burst into tears, and George and I looked at her in alarm.

"I'm so sorry, but I so wished that this war could be put behind us. It has caused so much pain and misery and death. George, please don't sing that song again around me. If only we could regain the love and happiness that we had before the war began. My dad died at the Second Battle of Bull Run and with his death, it killed my mother and left me homeless. If it weren't for the goodness of the restaurant giving me lodging and food, I don't know what I'd have done."

She burst into tears again.

I held her close in my arms and kissed the tears from her cheeks.

"George, I guess that's all for tonight. We'll sing again, but songs that will cheer and bring happiness," I said.

"Melody, I didn't mean to bring any unhappiness to you, but considered the song as words to chuckle at in the way they were written. We love you all and don't want you to be unhappy. I won't sing that song again," George said.

I knew, however, that the song revealed what most Texans thought of the reconstruction period. George had spent a lot of time to memorize the lines. George and I stood on the vast front porch of the hacienda and talked at length of the reconstruction and its effect upon the South, and especially Texas.

George was a well-read man and had read whatever he found. He began talking earnestly, sharing his thoughts with me on the plight of the black man.

"The black man has been set free, and countless numbers of

them have been testing their freedom and causing great fear to many a former owner. There's been an uprising in Haiti, and the South saw that nothing could keep blacks from uprising here. Much of this fear was due to former owners' conscience bothering them, but as that song states, we were subdued but we're not beaten. We wanted the old way of life, and the greatest assets of the South were land and labor. But the black supplied the labor, and what if the black wouldn't work? The Northern carpetbagger has come down here to remake the South and steal our land. Political problems have plagued us, for whoever has taken up arms against the Union cannot vote as a delegate. A lot of the slaves couldn't read and thus were illiterate, but still were made delegates by the carpetbaggers. On the other hand, there were four Confederate generals, and five Confederate colonels among those elected to office in the South in spite of the 'iron clad' oath they were supposed to take indicating they'd not taken up arms against the Union. There were fifty-eight Confederate congressmen elected from the South to Congress, and many were not pardoned.

"In the early part of the war, 125,000 slaves were shipped to Texas for safekeeping. I must admit that the black man was mistreated in this state. If he was ill, there was no master to care for him and give him free medicine. If he was old, he had to steal or beg to stay alive. The destruction left by Sherman and Grant's armies caused even more difficulty to the poor, white, and black alike. There just was no food to share with one another. When plantations were reestablished, the black man worked for nothing. Sometimes he worked just to live. Education was held back from the black man under the old assertion 'learning will spoil the nigger for work,' and then there was the general opinion that 'you cannot make the Negro work without physical compulsion.'

"Black schools set up by the North had teachers who taught their students such songs as *John Brown's Body* and *Hang Jeff Davis to a Sour Apple Tree.* Do you think we can rebuild our state built on ignorance and hatred? I can't see it," said George.

"It is a real problem," I managed to answer. "I heard that those plantations that mistreated the black man have their produce rotting in the field. Those who treated him in a Christian manner found it worked well for both of them. What would happen here if I hired a few black families and paid them to work as I pay my cowboys? Would it cause disharmony among us? We could use some field hands to put up hay and plant and tend gardens. George, all men were created equal, and I believe that. Let us try to overcome the hatred that exists here in Texas and try to treat both races alike. I have tried to make peace with the Indian, so why not with the black man?

"Melody has taught us the correct spirit. No one wants war and hatred. It's a terrible thing. 'Do unto others as you would have others do unto you' is not scripture, but it makes for a Christian spirit," I said.

•

In her fifth month of pregnancy, a traveling preacher came by and visited the ranch. I was interested, for he was of the same belief as a little congregation outside of Orange near the Barboursville Plantation. That little congregation had been established in 1850. They practiced New Testament theology and immersed people (and I was one of them) in the Rapidan River. The preacher had a two-week meeting at our ranch, and most of the cowboys attended, as did Melody, Matt, Bess, and I. We learned some gospel songs and, at the end of the week, the preacher took Matt, Bess, Melody, and five cowboys to the Colorado River, where he immersed them all.

The event caused all to have joy in our hearts and we met together in the hacienda each Sunday and sang, studied, and took communion. Revival was in Texas, and our preacher joined others and evangelized the whole area. I sent the preacher with Amos to the Kiowa tribe, where he spent several weeks with a lot of success. I paid Amos to go along and be an interpreter. I heard that Causes to Laugh and the other women of Wolf Fang's household all embraced Christianity. Causes to Laugh understood me better after she had been taught about Christian marriage.

Melody became more beautiful than ever to me as she became larger with child. The Spirit of God, which she now had in her life, caused her to radiate an inner light, which everyone noticed. She went out of her way to wait on her friends and loved ones. The cowboys all saw this and loved her like a little mother. Bess saw it and joined her in sharing love with all around them. Home became a place of love and concern for one another. Matt became a good earthly dad to us all, and he and I shared the responsibility of fatherhood.

•

Melody woke me in the middle of the night.

"My husband, it's time. Call Erma and Bess; I feel I'm about to give birth to our first child."

I ran and banged on Bess's door, and then ran for Erma. They both seemed as excited as I. Even the cook was out of bed and building a fire in the kitchen stove. He put on a lot of water and made plenty of coffee. Melody had a high pain level and was very considerate of us all. She was calmer than all of us, and smiled at our excitement. Two hours later, I heard a child cry and sat down at the kitchen table and gave thanks. Matt was there and grinned at me. Two minutes later, I heard a second cry, and Matt and I looked at each other. "You don't think… nah, that's the same child, but the cry was not as loud," said Matt.

Then we heard a chorus of sound as the little melodies sang together. Erma came in and held up two fingers.

"A boy and a girl. Mother is doing well."

"Can you believe that? God has blessed us with a son and another Melody," I said.

Matt pounded me on the back. "Congratulations," he said.

I could hear the cook out in the bunkhouse telling the news. I went to our bedroom door, and Bess had one of the babies, washing and cleaning him. She was dressing him in baby clothing, and when she saw me, she turned so I could get my first glimpse of our son. He was red as a beet and was agitated, for he was attempting to cry and had his fist in his mouth. His eyes appeared to be a dark blue, and he had my dark hair.

"He's a big baby," remarked Bess. "Want to hold him, Dad?"

She showed me how to support his back, and I held him in my big hands.

"Golly," I managed to say.

Erma came in with our daughter. The child was throwing her arms and kicking. Erma watched me as I handed my son back to Bess and reached for my daughter. Her eyes were lighter than my son's and her hair was lighter in color.

"A spitting image of Melody," said Bess as she looked on.

Erma agreed.

I held my daughter and admired her tiny features. I fell in love with both of my children the first time that I saw them. I carried the daughter into our bedroom. Melody was wet with perspiration, but was smiling when she looked up at me and I laid our daughter on her arm. The little child wanted to nurse and I watched her mother make arrangements.

"Great job, Melody."

I reached down and kissed her.

Tears ran down her cheeks from her lovely blue eyes.

"God has been good to us, my husband."

And so it was that William and Cheryl McDowell became a great part of our lives. I had a huge box of cigars, and I went to the bunkhouse, where I found a smiling group of cowboys. They all crowded around and wished the little ones a lot of love and congratulations to their old man. It wasn't long before the whole bunkhouse was filled with cigar smoke. They cranked my hand and beat me on the back. Their love was genuine and their actions jovial. Amos rode in and added his congratulations. He lit up one of the cigars and sat down on one of the bunks.

"Man, do I love these things!" he said, as he looked the cigar over. "Boss, have one child at a time rather than twins," he chided. His thoughts centered on extra cigars.

GARCIA ATTACKS AGAIN!

It was in the first week of November, 1867, the trees still had their colors. Nights were cold but autumn had not given way to heavy frost. The cowboys were busy putting up their late hay crop. I was a new dad and the twins were a week old.

"How does the ranch up north look?" I asked.

"I was so excited that I just forgot all about my report to you. Bud and I found evidence that we've some Indians living near the box canyon," said Amos.

"Oh, tell me about it," I said.

"West of the box canyon and hidden well from anyone that would pass by, I found the recent butchered remains of a young steer. It looked to me like they saw Bud and me before we got there, and we ran them away from their supper. There were moccasin tracks of four Indians. It sure made my skin crawl, as I was sure that they were watching us. The fire was small, but there was some dry wood left, and the fire was still burning."

"When was this?" I asked.

"Last night," he answered.

Matt was standing right behind me and had heard the full report. "Sounds like Juan Garcia to me, son," said Matt. "How many were there?"

"Four had been at the fire, but there might have been a lookout that warned them in time. It sure ran shivers up my back to run onto their camp and not know they were there. I didn't see their horses or tracks of their horses. Up on that Cap Rock, a horse will not leave a track," Amos reported.

"I want to get that Indian, as he stays around here with one purpose in mind and that is to kill me or mine. I've three more to look out for with your help, Matt. Let's make a drive on them and try to catch them in that area. If we can see them, and with our Winchesters, we've a chance of bagging all of them."

Rex, Matt, Amos, and Bud, and half dozen cowboys sat around as I took pencil and paper and drew a sketch of the area.

Three'll go directly west from here and make a drive north up the Cap Rock. Four will go to the Colorado and ford it; and continue north and swing west to the edge of the box canyon. Amos, Matt, and I will drive straight north along the trail. We should flush out something, but they'll undoubtedly see us three on the trail. We've an advantage over them, as they've only old single shot guns. When you hear shooting, close in and we should bag a couple or we might get all of them. Fellows, we on the trail will be the bait. Good hunting, as I want this guy's hide."

Early in the morning, the three that headed for the Cap Rock started first. The group of four to cross the Colorado started next, and we gave them an hour head start before we started riding up the trail. It was a beautiful day, and we watched everything that might conceal anyone. We were about twenty yards apart and were a bundle of nerves as we moved. Amos was at the point, and then Matt and I were watching our back trail. We were approaching the south end of the box canyon, when Amos turned back toward us and fell from his horse, nearly at the feet of Matt. An arrow was in his back, but missed his lungs and was stuck in his shoulder blade. A second arrow swished past Matt. He saw movement and shot five times. I saw some dust coming up from our back trail, and I dismounted from the mare and tied her to a small tree and moved toward Matt and Amos.

I saw a half dozen Indians coming from the south behind us. They'd baited this trap by letting Amos and Bud see them. I lay down behind a tree and began to shoot as fast as I could into the advancing Indians. Matt added firepower, and Amos lay flat in the grass working with the arrow, trying to remove it. The arrow had hit the shoulder bone and had not penetrated deeper, but was through the fleshly part of his shoulder. He broke off the feathered end of the arrow and felt for the arrow head. He pushed and the arrow head came on through just under his collar bone. Matt bent over him and pulled the arrow on through. There was a lot of blood, so Matt applied pressure and took off Amos' shirt and used it to bind up the wound.

I reloaded my gun and moved to a tree to our right in order to try to keep Indians from encircling us.

"Here they come!" I said.

I fired with deadly accuracy into the advancing Indians. Several lay in front of us, and then I saw him. It was Juan Garcia, and he was running toward me with a six-gun in his good hand. He saw me just as I shot into him. I shot again and again, and knew I'd not have Juan to worry about anymore. Hearing the shooting, the group of cowboys from the east and west converged into the battle area.

Suddenly, there were several cowboys firing, as our boys now had the Indians surrounded. The battle was fierce, but we had greater firepower, and soon it was over. Twenty braves lay in front and around us. Amos was sitting up and looking at Juan Garcia. Amos took his knife and cut from the front of Juan's forehead around to the back of his head. Amos was weak, but he'd planned for this day for a long time. With his good hand, he grabbed the lock of greasy hair and jerked hard. The scalp popped as the flesh and hair gave way from Juan's skull. Amos gave the war cry of the Kiowa brave and lifted the scalp for all to see.

"I always thought he was more Kiowa than white," Matt whispered to me. "We've avenged my daughter."

I nodded that it was all over. We counted noses and found one short.

"Where's Bud?" asked Rex. "He was with me back there."

Rex retraced his steps and found Bud with an arrow through his chest. I sat with my head in my hands. I'd lost a man and had a good friend almost killed because I'd sought revenge. I put Bud's body on his horse, and we bound Amos's wound tighter and headed for home. It was a good thing the Apache had no semi-automatic rifles as we had, or several of us would've been killed.

We were back home by dark, and there was a scout waiting on the trail watching for us. I smiled, for the cowboys were beginning to think like a smoothly operated military unit. I sent a cowboy to Amos's wife with the news that he'd been hurt, and Erma took off the blood-covered and saturated bandages and replaced them with clean ones. Amos was in good spirits in spite of the pain. The cowboy returned that night with Amos's wife. She took over caring for her husband.

The next morning, I took Bud's body into town and was followed by all of the cowboys. Bud was buried by his parents in the cemetery at Big Spring. We had lost yet another of our close-knit family.

I held Melody tight as I told her the results of the battle, and that we wouldn't have to worry about Juan Garcia again.

"Poor Delight was scared to death of that man. Juan ruined our happiness, and now it is all over! I had to kill him for the kids and your safety," I said as I held Melody and she wept softly.

Amos and his wife went home three weeks later. He was doing well and was sure to recover fully. This made me happy, for Amos was more than an employee; he was a true friend. But he was not a Christian and that worried me. Two weeks later, Amos was back at the ranch to work.

TROUBLE AT BIG SPRING

"Boss, we just got rid of one problem, Garcia. and we've something else to worry about. Robbie had to be turned lose. The one witness that could've put the blame on Robbie was found shot in one of the alleys. The Crosby killing is now self-defense and Robbie will walk free. That Jody is trying to talk up trouble between you and the carpetbaggers, saying you were a major in the Confederate army and should be run out of this area. There's someone else that has money who wants your place. That's the way I understand it," said Amos.

"Those four walls at home were closing in on me; I had cabin fever," declared Amos "I had to get out of there, so I went to the Last Chance Saloon; that's where I got my information."

"That part about someone with money being behind most of this trouble? Where did you get that information?" I asked.

"A gambler friend of mine that's in there a lot of the time told me," he said.

"He told me the same thing while I was a ranger," I said. "I wonder what part the gambler has in this. Why would he want to help us?" I replied.

Amos and I approached Matt about the gambler. Matt smiled and said,

"He was with the rangers when we all entered the Confederate army. The entire ranger group was named the Eighth Texas Cavalry and we fought first under Colonel Terry, who was killed in Kentucky, and we were under Lubbock, Wharton, and Thomas Harrison. We fought at Shiloh, and Fallen Timbers, and took Murfreesboro, and fought Yankee cavalry through Georgia. I feel our victories may well be the reason why we weren't returned to police action when the war was over."

"Then there are other reasons for your being dispersed rather than permitted to service as you were before the war. Texas voted against the ratification of the 14th amendment and only cast five votes for the amendment of the Constitution," I said.

"That gambler was there and fought right through with us and didn't want to surrender. I feel that he's doing what he's doing to try to help the citizens of the land against those carpetbaggers," continued Matt.

I thought of it and had to agree with Matt.

"I understand that several parcels of abandoned land have been confiscated by various Northern soldiers and some black people," said Amos.

"Now's the time to find out who this finance man is, check the ownership of those parcels, and who holds the paper on the finances," I said.

"I'll do that tomorrow," said Matt.

Early the next morning, Matt, supported by Amos, arose early and left for the real-estate office. Amos stood watch while Matt dug into the records and shook his head and said, "Well, I'll be."

The two men were careful in their work, not to be seen, for they didn't want any fanfare. They did not want the carpetbaggers to know of their quest for information. Matt brought his report in to me.

"John Kirby's name was on all the papers, but I wonder if Robert Duncan is not into it too. John Kirby is the manager at the bank and was Delight's boss. Yet, what could he do without Mr. Duncan knowing what was going on? Where did the money come from if it's not Robert Duncan behind it?" asked Matt.

"Where did John Kirby come from?" I asked.

"He came into this area when I was at war," said Matt.

"How long have you known Robert Duncan?" I asked.

"I think he came about the same time too," added Matt.

"I'd sure like to see our captain and his detail back in this area again. I believe he's sympathetic with the home folk of Texas. He might not be able to do anything militarily, but he might be able to give us some sound advice," I said.

"While I was at the real estate office, I looked up the ownership of that parcel consisting of about one thousand acres that runs up into that valley. The plat indicates it's Parcel B of the Spanish grant owned by Don," said Matt.

"You're kidding me, aren't you?" I said, surprised.

"He didn't say that he had another parcel. It's no wonder that Rex said they had cattle on that parcel. Let's send Rex to Mexico and see if Don wants to sell that parcel for three dollars an acre. I have that much, and it'd be a good buy. You can use your $700 to build a nice house on that property, and we can ranch both parcels together," I said.

"Sounds great!" said Matt.

"We'd better grab that land before Kirby or Duncan finds out about it and claims it as abandoned land and steals it away from Don. I'd hate to have them as our neighbors," I continued.

I questioned Rex as to the whereabouts of Don's Mexican ranch. Rex told me that he had taken horses to the ranch, when he worked for Don. I explained to Rex that I needed someone to carry a message to Don and would he go? The French were patrolling the border and there would be some danger involved in reaching Don's Mexican ranch. Rex agreed to go.

I sent Rex down into Mexico the next day with a written proposition regarding the selling of Parcel B of the tract.

He was gone for two weeks, but came back with a signed contract. Don would come to the hacienda to close the deal; he was more able to cross the border. Matt and I waited anxiously at my hacienda; Amos returned home.

I rode to town and got $3,000 in cash from my account. Mr. Kirby was very inquisitive regarding the cash and wanted to know when I was returning to the hacienda and to give his regards to Melody. I wondered whether he was planning some way to steal my $3,000.

I rode by to check on Amos and found him at home. He was smiling, for his father-in-law, Wolf Fang, was riding to meet him so that his daughter could spend some time at his village. I told him the fears that I had about carrying that much cash back home.

"Why it won't be out of his way but a few miles to escort you back to the ranch. I think I'll go along with you just to see the fun," Amos said.

Wolf Fang and twenty-five of his braves met Amos and his wife three miles north of town. They all were glad to see me and saluted me with their greetings. Amos spoke to Wolf Fang with the request of escorting me back to the ranch and told him that there may be trouble. It pleased the old chief that he could help the hunter and great white warrior. He carried his ten-gauge shot gun, which was very dear to him.

We started along the trail, and he sent scouts ahead and had two to trail us. We were near the five mile mark when the front scouts returned with information that there were six white men behind trees along the trail. He sent ten braves to the left and ten braves to the right and made sure his shotgun was loaded with heavy loads. The scouts went slightly ahead and stopped us on the trail. They spoke to their chief and pointed ahead. He called like a quail and the twenty Indians all converged on the area. Wolf Fang gave the signal, and we charged up the road. The six carpetbaggers made the mistake of shooting at the braves. Wolf Fang pulled one trigger and blew a renegade out of a tree. He spoke with glee in the Kiowa tongue, and Amos burst out laughing. Amos turned to me and said, "He said, 'big turkey.'" Amos laughed.

I had my Winchester at work, and we ran the five up the trail to the north. Lying on the ground was Jody Williams with his leg caught in the fork of the tree, where he'd been watching for me as I came along the trail. Wolf Fang's "turkey" still had his eyes swollen, but the buck shot had torn most of his head away. We left him where he'd fallen, and I thought it best for me to return to town to tell the marshal just what'd happened. I told Amos to stop at the ranch and go to the bunkhouse and tell Rex to send me a half dozen of our better men with six-guns. I wanted to have the $3,000 when Don came to close the sale, but thought I could go see the marshal and be square with him and not have him coming after me at the ranch. I rode to the livery and left my horse with orders to put him in one of the stalls at the rear, and that I'd need him early in the morning.

I walked to the hotel carrying my saddlebags with the $3,000, which I put in the hotel safe. I got my old room, which faced the street, checked my guns, and walked through the alley to the edge of town. I watched who went into the Last Chance Saloon and felt that about all of the carpetbaggers were still on the trail and trying to stay clear of the Indians. I stood away from the lights that might highlight me and waited in the shadows, watching the road.

It must have been two o'clock when I saw the five slowly moving into town. They looked like a dog that had been running sheep. They didn't have Toby's body, so I wasn't worried that they'd have some story concocted to cause me trouble. I knew exactly who they were. There was Robbie, the two Kansas gunslingers, Mr. Kirby, and Mr. Duncan. They stopped at the Last Chance and talked awhile, and then Mr. Kirby and Mr. Duncan went on into town and Robbie and the Kansas gunslingers went into the saloon. I sat there a few minutes watching Mr. Kirby and Mr. Duncan, and I decided to wait until they separated and I'd approach Kirby first.

Mr. Duncan said good night to the bank manager and went into his house, which was the largest building in town. Mr. Kirby was a widower and lived on Main Street, east of the bank. Mr. Duncan and Mr. Kirby had spoken in low tones to each other just long enough for me to get around them unseen and to beat Mr. Kirby to his house. He took his horse to the livery, unsaddled him, and turned him into his rented stall.

"Hello, Mr. Kirby," I said, as he came out of the stall.

My soft voice must've been the last thing he expected to hear, for he jumped back and made a choking sound. His face was lined with fear and his eyes bulged from his head. I was about to tell him that I knew what he'd done, but he grabbed at his throat, coughed, and gasped, and then fell face forward into the sawdust of the livery barn.

I checked his pulse, and detected a very faint pulse. Should I call the marshal? Maybe I should get the doctor first, but I didn't know where the doctor lived. I went to Matt's old house and banged on the door until the marshal appeared with gun in hand and told him that Mr. Kirby was lying in the livery barn, but still had a faint pulse. I told him that I didn't know where the doctor lived. The marshal quickly dressed, and came hurrying into the street, and made for the doctor's office and then to a bungalow at its side. It wasn't long before the doctor came with his kit, and I met them at the livery barn.

"He's dead. His face is black, and it looks like a massive heart attack. You find him?" he spoke to me.

"I met him as he was coming out of the stall and he fell right at my feet," I told them the truth.

"If a guy has to die, I guess that's the way to do it. You sure don't linger when you've one of those. I wonder where he'd been in those clothes this time of night?" asked the doctor. "Sheriff, I had him as a patient concerning his heart problems. I'll get Lawson's funeral parlor to come and get him. It is on my way home, and they'll need a death certificate anyway."

The marshal started to move toward home and said good night, but I stopped him. We went on to the jail, and I told him the full story of what had happened. I told him about Toby being shot out of the tree after the bandits had fired on the Indians first. I told him where to find his body. As he questioned me, he understood that Mr. Kirby was in on it and was happy that I hadn't shot the man.

"That would've really caused a stink, as we're under marshal law now and the Federal troops would be here; you, Tom, would be in trouble," he said. "They are questioning everything and everyone under these reconstruction laws. General Sheridan is a real ass. Excuse my French," he said, for he knew I didn't swear. "I'm just a figurehead and have no authority as a marshal. President Johnson is going to get kicked out of office before this is all over. You know anything about Sheridan?" asked the marshal.

"He was the Commander of the U.S. Cavalry in the eastern section, and I saw him at Appomattox. He is only about five and one half feet tall, and they called him 'Little Phil.' He was cavalry commander of the Army of the Potomac and helped cut off our retreat from Richmond. I understand that he worked his way up from a lieutenant to a major general during the war. He has restricted former confederate soldiers from having the power to vote, among other things. I also know that he'd selected General Charles Griffin as his subordinate here in Texas. Griffin was responsible for kicking out James Throckmorton as our governor because he was a Confederate, even though we voted him in. I also heard that Little Phil didn't care much about Texas. He said, 'If I owned Texas and hell, I would rent out Texas and live in hell.'"

"I believe in a heaven and a hell, and I believe that if he lived a full minute in hell, he would surely change his mind," I said with a chuckle.

"That's the man, all right!" agreed the marshal.

"Marshal, what should I do about the robbery attempt? I know Mr. Duncan, those two Kansas gunslingers, and Robbie were there. I would like to go with you to retrieve Toby's body in the morning. Maybe there is some proof that we might find," I said.

"Sure thing, Tom. Let's hit the bed for a little sleep; then get started tomorrow before the sun comes up. I'll see you at the restaurant at 6:00," said the marshal.

I walked through town to the hotel. That bed felt mighty good to me as I crawled in and blew out the lamp. Five-thirty came just two hours later.

•

Without Melody, the restaurant was just not the same, for they had another waitress; and who could replace Melody? The cook came out, and I answered several questions regarding my Melody. The cook was an ugly old man, but his heart was in the right place, and he was like a dad to Melody.

The marshal came in, and he had a cup of coffee with me, as he'd eaten at his house before he'd left.

Ebony was glad to see me, and the livery man had him fed and ready for the road. I paid the man, telling him I wasn't sure if I'd be there for another night or not.

I saw buzzards in the tree before we got to Toby, but they'd been feeding on him. The marshal was no fool and went to work pointing out the various positions of the bandits and studied their footprints. He picked up two cigarettes from one place and pointed out that they weren't handmade ones, but an expensive brand and knew of only one man who smoked them and who could afford them.

"These put the spike right in the heart of Mr. Duncan," he said, as he put the butts in an envelope and carefully placed them in his shirt pocket. "These prints belong to Robbie, for there isn't anyone that I know who has that large a shoe. These other two are pointed cowboy boots and are dressy like those worn by the Kansas gunslingers," he continued. "I think we got them, and these should hold up as proof in case you need them," he smiled.

"Let's get out of here in case they come by for Toby's body," I said.

I watched the trail for a few minutes just to be on the safe side. Our trip back to town was uneventful, and we were careful, lest we run into someone on the trail. My help should be here by noon, so I stayed at the marshal's office and waited for them.

"How are you going to handle it?" the marshal inquired.

"I've a couple of good gunmen coming that I want to cover my backside, and I'm going to approach the four bandits together if I find them together, or one at a time. I'm going to call them out before good witnesses and make a citizen's arrest. I want you there when I confront Mr. Duncan."

"Sounds right to me," he said. "I hope none of them fought for the North, as we might run into a snag with the blue bellies," said the marshal.

I rode Ebony to the Last Chance Saloon, but I saw no familiar outlaw horse or horses with the TM brand. I tied Ebony with a slip knot in case I had to get away from there in a hurry and stood a second or two at the door bats, looking in. The gambler was there, as well as a couple I didn't know standing at the bar. I walked in and sat at the table with the gambler and was careful to sit with my back to the wall.

"Want to try a hand with me?" he asked. "I need to talk to you, so we can play just to be social."

"I heard awhile ago that we lost our bank manager and you found him," he said as he shuffled the cards.

"Mr. Kirby died right in front of me over at the livery station. Doctor said he had a massive heart attack."

"Too bad it wasn't Mr. Duncan; he's the man that I told you to watch. He's the money behind all these killings and stealing land. I'm sure you know that."

He didn't lift his eyes to me as he spoke but just continued to examine the cards in his hands. I remembered what Matt had said about the gambler being with the rangers and fighting through the war and not wanting to surrender. I laid my cards on the table and said, "Gin."

He smiled at me and said, "Good hand, but wrong game; we're playing poker."

"Six men tried to rob me yesterday on my way home. There was Mr. Kirby, Robbie, and two Kansas gunfighters, as well as Toby. Kiowa friends were with me. Toby took a shot at Chief Wolf Fang, so now Toby is dead and Kirby died later of a heart attack. I'm here to see Robbie and the Kansas gunmen, but I don't have a plan on how to handle Mr. Duncan," I explained, never moving my gaze from the saloon door.

The gambler looked at me over his cards.

"I've some friends that want him. I won't say who they are, but they wear white sheets at night, if you know what I mean. A week ago, there was a cross burned on Duncan's front yard, and apparently he didn't get the hint."

"The KKK, eh? I heard something about them. I was told that KKK was the sounds made when a rifle was being loaded and ready to fire. I also heard that it's a term that came from China, and someone else said it came from Mexico. Who knows, eh? I heard it started at Pulaski, Tennessee by some unemployed Confederate veterans and spread from there. What is the scoop on them?" I asked.

"They've their reason for being. They're just trying to fight back against these reconstruction laws that favor the North against the South. If you give the KKK the opportunity, we'll run Mr. Duncan out of town or worse. We all feel that he paid to get young Crosby killed by Robbie.

Young Crosby and Cathy, daughter of Mr. Duncan, were interested in one another but Mr. Duncan didn't want Cathy to associate with Crosby. He wanted Cathy to marry someone with money and prestige. Cathy had her own mind, and met young Crosby in private places.

Duncan had warned Crosby to leave her alone, or else."

"Look, my friend, I'm not in any murder plot and would go along with you if he was just run out of town. If what you say about Cathy is true, then Duncan shouldn't get by with murder. We sure don't need citizens like that perched like vultures waiting to pounce on some innocent person," I said.

"I guarantee you that we'll not kill him, but we'll scare him half to death and may tar and feather him. He'll be gone from these parts back to where he came from," said the gambler. "If there's a way to get the truth out of him about Crosby and he's guilty of murder, then there are some in the KKK that'll lynch him. And I mean big time!"

"Try not to harm his daughter Cathy, as she seems a fine young lady." I said.

We shook hands, and I laid my cards down with a full house of three aces and two queens.

"Would I have won?"

"Good hand!" He turned his cards over and had four Kings. "But not good enough," he said.

"See why I never gamble?" I remarked.

I took Ebony back to the livery stable and went back to the hotel. I was sleepy, for I had very little sleep the night before; I opened the window, and laid down with my Colt in its holster. I slept through lunch and was awakened by a light tapping on the door.

"Who's there?" I asked as I held my Colt.

"It's us, Boss!" spoke a familiar voice.

I opened the door and Matt, George Cavenaugh, Rex, Slim Wilkins, and a young gunfighter that was one of the last five I hired after the raid on the hacienda by the name of Johnny Travis, all entered. They sat while I told them my plan to go to the Last Chance Saloon and accuse the three of attempted robbery. I only wanted my men to back me up and watch my back for me, and to especially watch the Kansas gunslingers, for I was mostly after Robbie for killing the ranger boy.

"These three bandits don't know you, George, or Slim, but they may know you, Rex, so I want Rex and Matt to be just outside and watch who comes and goes," I ordered. Then, completing my plans, I said, "George and Johnny, you go first and get a good location so that you can watch what is going on. When I call them out, if you want to step up with me, Slim, then come on, but I don't want anyone shot in the back. I want the witnesses that see this to know they're bandits and killers and I'm calling them out for that reason. I must let them draw first."

"Boss, I'm really not a gunman, but just a kid that needed a job and lied to get it," said a blushing Johnny Travis.

"Draw your pay not because you aren't a fighter, but because you lied to us," said George. "Stay out of the saloon or you might get yourself killed in there."

"I'll step through those doors at the right time and stand beside you," said Slim.

"George, you go first and we'll give you five minutes head start. We'll all walk over," I said.

George walked on to the saloon full of drinking cowboys and townspeople. He entered and immediately recognized all three of the robbers as they sat at a corner table playing cards. George stood at the bar to the left of the three outlaws. They turned as I entered. I heard Slim and Rex stop at the door of the saloon.

"Robbie," I spoke up in a very clear sharp tone, "you are a robber, a murderer, and a no-account carpetbagger down here to kill and steal."

I got the attention of the entire room, and I heard someone say, "That's Tom McDowell who cleaned out the restaurant the other night and gave Jody Williams the beating of his life with one punch."

"Oh, you're that ranger's friend. Fellows, I've wanted to get a chance at him," said Robbie to his friends.

There was a rush to get out of the line of fire and the front wall of the saloon was cleared. Rex was watching over the top of the swinging front door and Slim pushed open the door and moved up on my right side.

"Guns or fists?" I asked.

George moved away from the bar and drew the attention of the gunmen.

"You in this too?" asked one of the gunmen of Slim and George.

"Just here to make sure you keep your snotty nose out of it," Slim drawled.

"Only need one gun and one shot," said Robbie as he drew.

His gun cleared the holster when my gun appeared in my hand. Robbie was terrified as he stared into the barrel. His mouth fell open, but I didn't fire. It was not Robbie I saw, but the terrified look of a young soldier dying as the result of my rifle fire in the battle of Bull Run. My gun wavered and Robbie's face changed to one of glee. He started to raise his gun.

"Shoot, Boss! He'll kill you!" screamed Rex.

Still, I didn't move. A gun exploded to my right, followed by another farther to my right. I saw the smiling face of Robbie change to a look of amazement and a blue hole appeared in the middle of his forehead. The 44 bullet bounced him off the bar onto the floor, and he was dead before his fall was complete. The Kansas gunmen also tried to draw and managed to get their guns from their holsters, but were shot dead center.

"You all right, Boss?" asked Slim Jenkins, as he holstered his navy Colt. He turned to George, who was watching the effect the shooting had on others. George's Colt 44 was in his hand and smoke was curling from the barrel.

"Thanks for the backing," said Slim.

"This is the guy that shot my young ranger from the side and didn't give him a chance. You all saw that he drew first," Matt stated.

"Those aren't gunfighters. Those are sneaking blue belly carpetbaggers," said Slim.

"You named them right, cowboy!" yelled one of the townspeople.

"Those three were after Crosby's farm after their last boy was killed," replied another.

So, it was over. My men were around me, but didn't ask why I didn't shoot.

"Anyone see what happened here?" asked the marshal, and five stepped up to describe what they'd seen. All were local Texans and all told the truth. There would be others who would come into town to take advantage of the unfair reconstruction laws and try to steal or take land from some unfortunate family that'd lost their men folk in the war.

"Come to my office, as I need a written statement from all of you as to what happened," said the marshal. The five witnesses all followed the marshal, and all agreed on the written statement and signed it.

"I'm sorry, George, Slim. I feel I left you in a tight spot. Robbie suddenly looked like the first young soldier that I killed at Bull Run, and I just couldn't lift my gun against him to save my life."

•

Rex, George, Slim, and I stopped by the Last Chance on our way back to the ranch. I wanted to hear from our gambler friend what people were talking about in the town of Big Spring. We joined the gambler, who was sitting at his usual table. Then, without us saying a word, the gambler gazed at the ceiling and began in a near whisper,

"The KKK paid a visit to Mr. Duncan last night; a cross was burned on his front yard. Mr. Duncan tried to resist. He got out his gun, but was overpowered. Hot tar was poured on him and chicken feathers were stirred into the cooling mess. 'This is being done by your neighbors for stealing, Mr. Duncan. You gather your family and get out of here or we'll cut your throat or hang you next time. If we knew for sure you'd killed young Crosby then we'd hang you now' said one of the sheet-covered men. Mr. Duncan has left Big Spring for parts unknown," said the gambler.

EPILOGUE

With the death of Garcia, the demise of Kirby, Robbie, Jody Williams, the Kansas gunmen, and Mr. Duncan's departure, peace came down like a mighty stream on Big Spring and the hacienda. Melody and I enjoyed the freedom of riding together. Danger of Indians and bandits was in the past.

Don Michael Lopez sold Matt and I the one thousand acres, and I paid three thousand dollars for it. Matt cut trees from the hills, and the TM ranch built him and Bess an attractive cottage.

Rex married Erma, and they moved north into the town of Amarillo; but they visited us often, and have a standing invitation to come whenever they wish.

William and Cheryl McDowell were blessed with another brother, Howard, and another sister, Katherine. They all were of excellent health; William and Howard had dark hair and gray eyes and were spitting images of their dad, whereas Cheryl and Kate had the large blue eyes and light brown hair of their mother. They all were raised to believe in Christ and to love one another. Melody taught them music and she sang along with them.

I hung up my "Golden Boy" Winchester, for it was a weapon of the times. A successor to the "Golden Boy" was the "gun that won the west," which was a slightly advanced Winchester.

I prayed many times for God's forgiveness as I thought of the many men I had killed. There were strangers that I killed in the war. I thought of the American aborigines that I had slain in battle. My thoughts went to some that I thought needed killing, and to those who killed my Delight and Paul. Still, it's not my place to take revenge. A soldier in Blue at the battle of Bull Run almost got me killed, but taught me with his life what the scriptures say in Romans 12:19, "Avenge not yourselves, but rather give place unto wrath: for it is written, Vengeance is mine; I will repay, saith the Lord." The basic reason the four of us from Orange joined Kemper's company A, was not slavery but anger. Of the four of us, only dad owned slaves. We were angry over how the North was treating us.

I'm training four little McDowells in the scriptures. I look at them and my lovely wife and I say, "I am blessed, indeed!"

My beloved Texas was readmitted to the United States on March 20, 1870. I was very happy when the carpetbagger rule was abolished in 1873. Dad, as I now habitually called Matt, was called to active duty in May of 1874 when the rangers were reorganized into six companies of seventy-five men each. Matt was to be a commander, but Bess wanted him at home. I was surprised when Matt turned down the offer to return to law enforcement. He wanted everyone to know that he was happy in ranching. I'd helped Matt and Bess to construct the home of their dreams, and Matt had entered into ranch life with joy and vigor. It wasn't long before Matt had paid me all the debt that he owed and got his own brand. His thousand-acre ranch became known as the MBD brand. Delight had wanted her name in our brand, and now Matt had put it in his own, which I'd made possible. I helped him in everything that I could to have a working ranch.

Matt shared his knowledge that he had of Mr. Duncan with the new Texas Rangers, and Mr. Duncan was tried and found guilty of killing young Deputy Crosby. Mr. Duncan was hung by the State of Texas in 1878.

Melody and I spent much time with Mom and Dad, and they looked on our four children as their own grandchildren.

Matt and I pooled our cattle drives and received some good contracts for beef sales at Fort Sumner, so the good times continued for the both of us. We found that there were companies that would contract to drive our cattle over the Dodge City or Ogallala trails to market.

The Houston and Great Northern Railroad companies, as well as several other companies, were busy buying right of way and laying track. By 1879 I learned that there were 2,440 miles of track laid in Texas. The coming of the railroad brought an influx of neighbors to us, and several smaller towns began to spring up. In 1880, there was the tenth census taken and our state of Texas had a population of 1,197,287 white and 393,384 black, but by the eleventh census of 1890, the population had grown in Texas to 1,745,935 white and 488,171 black.

One of the big problems we faced during the cattle years of mid 1850s and later years of the nineteenth century was "Texas Fever" in our cattle. The shipment of our cattle into some of the states in the North caused an epidemic of this fever, and some states quarantined our cattle. Matt and I were lucky. When "Texas Fever" endangered us, we quarantined our own stock, and our herds were spared large losses. It was found much later that the fever was caused by ticks.

Amos continued on with us, and he and his wife moved to the ranch. Since he hadn't taken up arms against the United States, he homesteaded one hundred and sixty acres adjacent to my ranch. We constructed them a home using native lumber, and they started a family of three. Her dad came and visited her often; whenever he was there, he'd come over to visit me. He loved my rum tobacco, which I kept especially for him. A few of my cowboys, including Rex, enjoyed the flavor too.

Wolf Fang and I would sit and smoke and relive the hunting experiences of shooting turkey and bison. Red Hand would come with his 12-gauge shotgun, and we'd hunt quail and turkey on my ranch. I acquired some excellent English Setters, which I trained to hunt both quail and turkey. Of course, I had to obtain the proper 12-gauge shot for Red Hand, as he had trouble buying the shells.

Causes to Laugh finally found the right man for her. She was taught Christianity by the same young preacher who'd held the two-week revival at our ranch. She became a leader among the women of her tribe and was taught to read the Bible by the missionary. Her thirst for knowledge was very strong, and she spent more and more time with the young minister. Causes to Laugh fell in love, and the minister asked her to marry him. She understood how important it'd been for me to stay true to my God and to keep myself for the right girl. She chided Amos that it wasn't mourning that kept me from her, but a righteous God. Amos agreed that love of God was the real reason.

Causes to Laugh and John Beasley were married, and he continued his work among the Kiowa; many of the tribe became Christians. When the tribe was required to move to a reservation, it was done without bloodshed.

Causes to Laugh gave birth to a child whom they named Ruth, who was the same age as Cheryl and William. Ruth had brown eyes like her mother and auburn hair. Ben was born ten years after Ruth and had the red hair of his dad. His Uncle, Red Hand, loved the boy like a father and taught him Indian lore and took him hunting and fishing,.

Rex went into business for himself when he, along with some others from Big Spring, formed a crew to take cattle north on what became known as the Western Trail. This cattle trail also became known as the Dodge City Trail. It followed some of the trail that we originally made when we delivered the cattle to the forts in New Mexico. The trail began at San Antonio and crossed the Red River at Doan's store and then straight north all the way to Dodge City, Kansas. Later, the trail was extended to army forts in Nebraska, Colorado, and Wyoming. I knew Rex to be honest and sincere, and took care of the cattle in the drive as he did when he worked for me.

Erma gave birth to two sons, and she would bring them to the hacienda to play with our children and keep Melody company while Rex was away. The boys had the black hair of their father and had his smile and disposition.

We used Rex also in our own drives, as did Matt.

George Cavenaugh stayed on as my ranch manager and eventually married one of the town girls and lived on our ranch. Slim Wilkins took over the job, which Matt gave up, of security boss. He was the only man that I wouldn't want to challenge with a six-gun. Other ranches were plagued with rustlers, but the fame of Slim Wilkins and my "Golden Boy," and the shooting of Juan Garcia discouraged them.

Melody made an excellent mother and wife. I loved her more

each day and we were very considerate of one another. She played her piano and taught her children.

Melody, you see, was named correctly. Melody caused a wonderful spirit of song and happiness wherever she went. She'd take the surrey into town and visit with the cook, and eventually bought a share in his restaurant. The purpose of the purchase was to help the cook financially, for he'd been such a great help to her when she needed someone. When I asked her why she sang and played her piano so much, she looked at me and said, "Husband of mine, don't the scriptures that you read so much say in Isaiah 23:16 to: *'Make sweet melody, sing many songs, that thou mayest be remembered'?*" The scripture was there but she had taken it out of its context. I knew what she meant and answered her.

"Oh my sweet Melody, there is a reason why you sing, for you have the wonderful Spirit of God in your heart," I said.

And who knew her better than I?

And so, that's the way that it was North of Big Spring!

LIVE

---

listen|imagine|view|experience

AUDIO BOOK DOWNLOAD INCLUDED WITH THIS BOOK!

In your hands you hold a complete digital entertainment package. Besides purchasing the paper version of this book, this book includes a free download of the audio version of this book. Simply use the code listed below when visiting our website. Once downloaded to your computer, you can listen to the book through your computer's speakers, burn it to an audio CD or save the file to your portable music device (such as Apple's popular iPod) and listen on the go!

How to get your free audio book digital download:

1. Visit www.tatepublishing.com and click on the e|LIVE logo on the home page.
2. Enter the following coupon code:
   fcdb-1a8d-937f-8d89-4fe5-c92b-a337-3714
3. Download the audio book from your e|LIVE digital locker and begin enjoying your new digital entertainment package today!